'You were a virgin.

'Rosie, I should regret what happened, apologise, but in all honesty I can't. You were so...' He paused, as if his aptitude for the English language had suddenly deserted him. His fingers slid from her jawbone and tracked gently down the side of her throat. 'Sensational.'

The intensity of his level silver gaze, the stark masculine beauty of his features, the touch of his hand against her skin make her feel helplessly dizzy. She wanted to hold him, to wrap her arms around him and tell him how swollen her heart felt, swollen with so much love she could hardly contain it. But his next statement made her go cold all over.

'As this was your first time, I don't expect you're protected.'

Her mouth dropped open. She hadn't given the matter any thought at all.

Diana Hamilton is a true romantic and fell in love with her husband at first sight. They still live in the fairytale Tudor house where they raised their three children. Now the idyll is shared with eight rescued cats and a puppy. But, despite an often chaotic lifestyle, ever since she learned to read and write Diana has had her nose in a book—either reading or writing one—and plans to go on doing just that for a very long time to come. This is her 40th book for Harlequin Mills & Boon®!

Recent titles by the same author:

HIS CONVENIENT WIFE
THE ITALIAN'S TROPHY MISTRESS
THE ITALIAN'S WIFE

THE SPANIARD'S WOMAN

BY

DIANA HAMILTON

First published in Great Britain 2003
Harlequin Mills & Boon Limited,
Eton House, 18-24 Paradise Road, Richmond, Surrey TW9 1SR

ISBN 0 263 83216 3

Set in Times Roman 10½ on 12¼ pt.
01-0303-46984

Printed and bound in Spain
by Litografia Rosés, S.A., Barcelona

CHAPTER ONE

SEBASTIAN GARCIA'S mood was blacker than a coalminer's finger-nails as he faced the rambling sixteenth-century façade of Troone Manor. His smoke-grey eyes narrowed then glittered with angry determination. He'd claw his heart out of his breast with his own hands before he'd allow Terrina Dysart to get her gold-digger's talons on his godfather's extensive property!

For the first time in his twenty-nine years a visit to the charming old house that had been like a second home to him for most of his life was lacking in anything remotely approaching pleasure.

The cold March wind pushed icy fingers through the sleek blackness of his hair, reminding him that his family home in Southern Spain and the village of Hope Baggot in the uplands of west Shropshire might as well be poles apart.

Firming his already hard jaw, he reached a leather suitcase from the back seat of the silver Mercedes and strode over the circular sweep of gravel to the main door where Madge Partridge was waiting to greet him. His tersely snapped, 'Is everything in hand?' wiped the welcoming smile from the housekeeper's lined face, and she took a flinching step backwards.

Silently cursing himself for losing his cool, he dredged up a smile. A lift of one ebony brow was enough to have his business staff jumping if the occasion demanded it. But dear old Madge was his godfather's housekeeper and she was only following Marcus's orders—as he himself was reluctantly doing. And making good and sure Marcus Troone got to see what Terrina really was, was his problem, not Madge's.

'Sorry,' he apologised through the smile he was doing his best to keep in place. 'I didn't mean to bite your head off.' He lifted wide, leather-coated shoulders in an expressive shrug. 'I've been driving through the night; put it down to that and forgive me?'

'Of course.' Briefly, Madge put a workworn hand to the side of his face, her gaunt features relaxing as she grumbled at him, 'You wouldn't take the easy way out and fly over in comfort, get a driver from the London office to meet you at the airport and chauffeur you here, not you!'

Her brown eyes glinted with affectionate amusement as he walked past her into the huge, raftered hall where a log fire was burning brightly in the stone fireplace. 'The first time you ever stayed here without your parents—you'd have been six years old—you decided that coming down to breakfast via your bedroom window and the wisteria would be more of a challenge than using the stairs. So nothing's changed, has it?'

The memory of the truly awe-inspiring scolding he'd received from Tia Lucia on that long-ago occasion made his heart dip with sadness. Marcus Troone and Sebastian's father, Rafael, had been business partners and Marcus had married Rafael's younger sister, Lucia. They had regarded themselves as one family.

Sebastian had spent long weeks every summer at Troone Manor, and life had seemed happy and uncomplicated.

But shadows had invaded the scene, invaded and deepened. To their sadness, his aunt and Marcus—who was also his godfather—had remained childless, and he had been approaching his eighth birthday when the unthinkable had happened and his lively, loving Tia Lucia had been stricken with multiple sclerosis. The next time he'd visited she'd been confined to a wheelchair, almost as helpless as a baby.

Two years ago Lucia had died and now Marcus, lonely and childless, was on the point of marrying a gold-digging witch!

'Not knowing exactly when to expect you, I held lunch back. It will be about an hour, so would you like coffee before you freshen up?'

With difficulty, Sebastian hauled himself out of the pit of his seething anger and grunted an affirmative to the housekeeper's question, dumping his case on the worn flagstones and following her through to the comfortably homely kitchen regions.

The whole place reeked of fresh emulsion. It made him shudder. Not the smell of the paint itself, but the implications. If Terrina got her hands on this property, the comfortable, slightly shabby ambience of what he'd always regarded as the essence of an English country house would be replaced by smart, over-decorated, expensive tat.

Not that he begrudged his godfather the happiness and companionship of a second marriage—Lord knows his role of husband had been reduced to that of dedicated carer for well over twenty years—but marriage to a greedy little harpy who would do anything, say anything, to get her hands on his enormous wealth and then, inevitably, break his heart—no way!

'Sir Marcus is more himself now?' Madge asked, motioning Sebastian to the old armchair at the side of the vast kitchen range as she busied herself with the coffee things. 'I was shocked, but not surprised, when he collapsed just before Christmas. He'd been working himself to a standstill since Lady Troone passed away, poor thing.'

'Much better,' Sebastian conceded as he accepted the coffee she handed him; strong, black and unsweetened, just the way he liked it. 'A few weeks on the warm shoreline below Jerez with my mother to cluck over him, and me, as his partner since my father's death, to report back on both the London and Cadiz ends of the business, and he's fighting fit again.'

'Must be, if he's gone and got himself engaged.'

He noted the questioning tone, the undercurrent of anxiety, understood exactly where she was coming from, but decided to ignore it. Faithful and loyal though the good soul was, there was nothing the housekeeper could do. It would be unkind to tell her of his own deep misgivings and add to her worries. It was his problem and, utterly distasteful though it was, he knew how he had to handle it. But, for the time being at least, he would comply with his godfather's request.

'The decorators have finished?' He deliberately changed the subject.

'Yesterday.' She sat at the central scrubbed pine table and ladled sugar into her milky coffee. 'Sir's instructions were just a plain, freshening-up job. No doubt his new wife will have her own ideas of how she wants to redecorate the house.'

Visions of expensive designer chic—stark, shiny and completely soulless—flooded his brain again. He quickly ousted them and asked, 'And the temporary staff?'

'Ah.' Madge's mouth turned down at the corners. 'Only two responded to the advertisement so it was Hobson's choice. Sharon Hodges from the village—you might have seen her around? Big, bulgy, mouthy lass. Knowing that feckless, lie-abed family, I insisted she live in for the full six weeks; that way I can make sure she gets out of bed and starts work on time. And the other girl comes from Wolverhampton. A little bit of a thing, she is. Looks as though a puff of wind would blow her over—I did explain there was a good deal of hard physical work involved, but if that bothered her she didn't say so. Come to think of it, she didn't say much, just that her mother had died a few months ago and she wanted a stop-gap job while she decided what she wanted to do. Name of Rosie Lambert. She'll be twenty the day after tomorrow, blushes if you so much as look at her and hangs her head as if she's got something to be ashamed of.

'Still.' Madge Partridge heaved a resigned sigh. 'Beggars can't be choosers. They both moved in yesterday and they've started on the bedrooms, getting rid of the paint splodges the decorators left. Quite frankly, I don't think either of them will be what I'd call satisfactory.'

'Leave them to me.' Sebastian gave her the benefit of his warmly confident smile. If anyone knew how to get the best out of hired staff, he did. Madge had enough on her plate and for the time being, until he worked out exactly how and when and with the least hurt he could wipe the scales from his beloved godfather's eyes, he would go along with his instructions.

'The whole place has been run down for years,' Marcus had confided. 'Madge can't cope with a place that size on her own and what help she has been getting from a village daily doesn't make much difference. My fault. I should have had a firm of cleaners come in regularly, but Lucia, bless her, was dead against it. She couldn't stand the upheaval and hated the thought of strangers touching her things. So hire a gang of live-in temporary domestics to get the place spotless before I bring Terrina back to organise the engagement party she's set her heart on. After we're married she can decide what she wants to do about staffing the place.' His smile had broadened into what Sebastian had described to himself as a grin besotted enough to earn the title of imbecilic. 'The first on her list of priorities will be a nanny!'

In the way of manipulative, greedy women the world over—and Sebastian had had enough experience of the breed to recognise one when he saw one—Terrina had quickly found her prey's Achilles' heel. Marcus's abiding regret was that his marriage had been childless. Armed with that knowledge, Terrina had allowed her sweetly confided desire to have a large family to become sickeningly repetitive.

Making a conscious effort to stop himself from scowling, Sebastian announced, 'Don't worry about it, Madge, I'll stick around long enough to make sure the show's well on the road,' before taking himself off to the room he'd always occupied on his visits there.

Rosie Lambert sat back on her heels and pushed a descending strand of long pale blonde hair out of her eyes with a rubber-gloved hand. It left a trail of scrubbing water down the side of her face. Two tears slid down her cheeks, adding to the mess. She could feel a huge sob building up inside her narrow ribcage as she fumblingly tried to mop her face on the sleeve of the giant brown overall Mrs Partridge had given her to wear.

She truly wished she had never come here, wished she'd never found the letter that had told her who her father was, wished she'd never listened to her friend and erstwhile employer, Jean Edwards.

It had been a quiet Monday morning in the street corner mini-market owned by Jean and Jeff Edwards. Rosie had been working there full-time since her mother's death and had gratefully accepted the invitation to move into the spare room in the living premises above until she found her feet. Anything to escape the flat in the high-rise block on the sink estate where she and Mum had lived for the past nineteen years.

'You won't want to work as a check-out girl and shelf-stacker all your life—not a bright girl like you,' Jean had stated unequivocally. 'You could even try to take the place at university you gave up when your poor mother became so ill.'

Rosie had had no idea about the direction her life would take. She'd been angry, saddened and confused since absorbing what her mother had told her a few days before her death, since finding that letter afterwards. Not a state of mind conducive to clear forward thinking. And, because her mother had refused to let her have anything to do with the other children who roamed the estate like packs of half-wild little animals, Rosie hadn't a friend in the world except Jean and her husband Jeff.

She'd needed to confide in someone and Jean had listened. Two months later, on that quiet Monday morning, the older woman had produced the local paper she'd taken from her sister-in-law's house in Bridgnorth when they'd been visiting the day before.

'I was just glancing through it and saw this. It's fate. Got to be. Read it.'

And there, in the Situations Vacant column, something that had made Rosie's heart emulate a steam hammer:

> Temporary live-in domestic staff required for six weeks from the beginning of March. Excellent pay and conditions. Apply Troone Manor, Hope Baggot.

Followed by a phone number.

'Apply,' Jean had advised when Rosie had got over her shock sufficiently to stop shaking. 'You needn't actually take the job, but getting interviewed would give you the chance to at least get a look at the village where your grandparents lived and where your mother was born and grew up. You could get a look at your father, too—there's obviously no doubt about Marcus Troone being the selfish wretch who got your poor mum pregnant, not from what you've told me—and decide whether you take to him enough to want to take it further. And, even if you loathe him on sight, he owes you big time. Stands to reason.'

Like the clown that she obviously was, Rosie had truly expected to be interviewed by Sir Marcus Troone himself and had steeled herself to decide whether she wanted to explain who she was, or whether she'd hit him with her handbag for treating her poor mother so badly and risk being charged with criminal assault.

Of course he wouldn't lower himself to interview a humble cleaner, she'd chided herself, when she'd faced Mrs Partridge over the kitchen table. And had gone on to remind herself bitterly that Sir Marcus would only notice an employee if she happened to be young, pretty and a likely pushover.

Towards the end of her life her mother had confessed that she'd fallen in love with the man who had fathered Rosie while working in the gardens of his home during the long summer break from the horticultural college she was attending. And, after finding the letter on the Troone Manor headed notepaper, that snippet had fallen neatly into place. Her grandfather had worked in the Manor's gardens; she knew that much. What would be more natural than that he should choose his daughter to help out during her summer break when temporary staff would be taken on to help with the extra seasonal work?

Her mother had gone on to confide that her lover had been married and that they'd both known that what they were doing was dreadfully wrong but had loved each other so much they simply couldn't help themselves.

A likely story! Rosie had thought, hanging her head

in case Mrs Partridge should see the burning mixture of anger and pain in her eyes and think she was demented. She knew her mother had adored her lover, but what kind of man would leave the girl he'd seduced—barely eighteen years old at the time—to abandon her career to care for the child he refused to acknowledge or support, to live out her life in borderline poverty?

And the wretch wasn't even here! During the interview it had been revealed that Sir Marcus was in Spain and would be returning in a few weeks' time with his new wife-to-be, which was why the neglect of years had to be swept, dusted and polished away.

At that point Rosie had known she should terminate the interview, apologise, and walk away. But doubts, and, let's face it, she told herself now as she bent to her task of locating the off-white spots of paint on the broad oak boards, the need to find out everything she could about her father and hope to goodness he wasn't as black as her imagination had painted him, had her dumbly accepting the offered temporary position.

A big mistake. She felt really sneaky and it wasn't a nice feeling.

'Hunt him down! He should know who you are,' Jean had said. But it was unworthy. Her mother had been wise enough to put the past behind her, accept that the father of her child was no part of her life, and in honour of her memory Rosie knew she should have done the same.

More tears threatened. Rosie sniffed loudly and started to scrub ferociously at a spot that stubbornly refused to budge.

* * *

Sebastian walked through the open door of his usual bedroom and did a double take at what appeared to be a mound of brown nylon fabric, the soles of a pair of beat-up plimsolls and a bucket.

The mound emitted a loudly prolonged sniff and a smile played at the edges of his mouth in instinctive male appreciation as a neat little backside began to sway to and fro as the scrubbing brush was wielded in a sudden burst of savage energy.

This was not the big, bulgy girl of Madge's description so it had to be the other. Rosie Lambert. That bobbing backside couldn't be called big by any stretch of the imagination. Neat, curvy and very, very feminine.

He cleared his throat brusquely to slap down his libido and gain her attention. Then widened his eyes as 'the little bit of a thing' scrambled to her feet as if she'd been shot, clutching her scrubbing brush in front of her in rubber-gloved hands.

The vulnerable beauty of her wide sapphire eyes stunned him. She'd been crying. Bright drops were tangled in her thick lashes and when the scarlet receded, leaving her delicately hollowed cheeks milky pale, he could see grubby streaks marring the perfection of her skin.

Compassion, or something very like it, stirred sharply inside him. Hadn't Madge said she'd recently lost her mother? What about her father, siblings? Such a little scrap of a thing needed someone to look out for her!

Surprised by the powerful intensity of his thoughts, he placed his suitcase at the foot of the bed, black brows meeting in a frown. Such fraternal feelings were totally unlike him and he didn't know where they were coming from. He'd naturally felt protective towards his mother and Aunt Lucia. And that was it. In his experience, the female of the species was pretty good at looking out for number one.

'You must be Rosie,' he stated softly when he became aware that his scowl was making the poor scrap quiver, his eyes drawn, for some reason, to her parted lips. Bee-stung? Rosebud? He searched for the most appropriate adjective and whimsically decided on kissable.

Dios! He was either losing his marbles or he had been without a woman for far too long! Plastering a smile that he hoped was reassuring on a face that felt oddly stiff, he introduced himself, 'I'm Sebastian Garcia. I'll be around for a while making sure that everything's as it should be when Sir Marcus returns.'

'You know my—' Rosie smartly zipped her mouth. Heaven help her—she'd been about to say 'father' and had only just stopped herself in time. Blushing hotly, she lowered her head and added, 'Employer?'

Oh, my, she didn't know what had come over her; she really didn't. When she'd heard that masculine attention-commanding throat-clearing thing she'd immediately and foolishly assumed that the father she had never known had unexpectedly returned.

Wild and conflicting emotions had propelled her upright at the speed of light and she'd found herself staring at the most compulsively attractive male she'd ever clapped eyes on. So heart-thumpingly sexy she just couldn't force her eyes off him.

Gorgeous smoky-grey eyes with unbelievable dark

lashes, midnight hair, a thin blade of a nose that made him look a real aristo and a wide narrow mouth that sent unaccountable shudders up and down her spine. Add a lean but powerful physique and a slight but oh-so-sexy Spanish accent and it was no wonder she was feeling a bit—overwhelmed.

'Marcus is my business partner, my godfather and a long-time family friend.' A slight smile curved the sculpted lines of that wicked mouth and Rosie felt her stomach turn over. A lump of irrational disappointment lodged behind her breastbone; she had hoped he was just another employee, more on her level, not a member of the wealthy, exalted clan she and her poor dead mother had been excluded from. Though why she should think that way, she had no idea. Except—

To her shame she felt another of those wretched blushes crawling over her face and dipped her head so that her hair, which had finally escaped its ponytail, fell forward and hid her burning cheeks. Trust her to have silly thoughts about a man who was so far out of her reach he might just as well be inhabiting a parallel universe, a man who had the kind of looks which only existed in female fantasies!

Sebastian grinned with wry amusement. Females who moved in his social circles didn't blush when spoken to. They bridled, pouted, husked, and sent explicit messages from calculating eyes. Rosie Lambert's reaction to him was a new and intriguing experience. And she had beautiful hair. It fell around her face like a waterfall of softest, palest silk and a curl of string, presumably used to tie it out of the way, was tangled up in the silky strands.

Ignoring the impulse to pluck the string away—she

would probably faint like a Victorian virgin if he so much as touched her—he heard her mumble, 'I'll get out of your way.'

Her slight body was trembling as she turned back to her bucket, her spine rigid with tension. Unaccountably, he had a compelling urge to ask why she was so uptight, try to help. Sensibly, he ignored it. She would probably run a mile if he became personal on such a short acquaintanceship. It would have to wait. Instead, he said blandly, 'No, please carry on with your work. It's got to be done and you won't be bothering me.'

Somehow Rosie found the strength to turn and look at him. He was shrugging out of his leather jacket, revealing a torso of utterly perfect proportions covered by a dark, fine wool sweater. And he had endless legs; sexily narrow hips. Her mouth ran dry and she couldn't breathe, because there was the strangest, most unnerving sensation of heat deep inside her.

And, for a big man—he had to be well over six feet tall to her diminutive almost three inches over five feet—he moved with surprising grace, she noted as he walked to the vast hanging cupboard to stow away his jacket.

Sebastian Garcia was the first man who had ever made her feel this weird, almost as if she no longer had any control over her body or her thoughts. But thankfully he hadn't noticed the way she was gawping at him or suspected the effect he was having on her, she told herself as she finally turned back to her bucket and dropped down on her knees.

As he'd said, her presence in what was obviously his bedroom didn't bother him. Why should it? She attacked the few remaining drops of dried paint with a violent surge of energy. She was just a cleaning lady—someone who, if she wasn't being given instructions, became completely invisible.

So admitting, even to herself, that he really turned her on, would be stupid. As stupid as coming here in search of a father who had never wanted her.

CHAPTER TWO

ROSIE sat on the edge of her bed, her shoulders slumped dejectedly. It was her birthday and she had never felt so lonely.

She had no problem with the fact that she had spent the whole day on her hands and knees; she was being paid as a cleaner, after all. She didn't want fuss or fanfares or piles of gift-wrapped goodies, nothing like that. It was the long evening ahead she dreaded.

She and Mum had always made birthdays special. There had been no money for fancy gifts but there had always been something extra nice for supper, a candle on the table and a bottle of inexpensive wine to share—an innovation that had appeared on her sixteenth birthday.

It was her mother she missed so dreadfully, her tired features magically seeming youthful and carefree again in the candlelight, her chatter and laughter.

A hard knot of anger turned her stomach upside down. It needn't have been like that, her mother taking any menial job she could find to support them, scrimping and scraping, making light of hardship, while her father lived in the lap of luxury here, completely unconcerned as to the fate of the girl he'd seduced, their baby.

As the anger threatened to pull her slender frame to pieces, she leapt to her feet and began to pace the small attic room she'd been given.

Growing up, she'd learned not to ask about her father. She had always got the same answer. 'We loved each other so much. But it wasn't to be.' Which had told her nothing, so she'd stopped asking, primarily because whenever she brought the subject up her mother looked so sad.

But a few days before her death, as if sensing her end was near, her mother had confessed, 'Your father never knew of your existence. I was still living with your grandparents and I left home as soon as I knew I was pregnant. He was married and if I'd told him I was expecting you he would have been put in a terrible position. So, as far as he was concerned, I just disappeared. I thought it best for all of us.' Her eyes had flooded with tears. 'I don't want you to think badly of him; I couldn't bear that. He was a fine man.'

Rosie hadn't believed that. She still didn't. She really would like to, but she couldn't. She was pretty sure her mother had been trying to put her lover in a better light just so her daughter wouldn't spend her life bearing a grudge against the man her poor mother had so obviously still loved.

Unconsciously, she put her hand to her breast. She could feel the pendant through the faded fabric of her T-shirt. Proof of her identity, she supposed, should she ever try to use it.

Her face went pale as she recalled how her mother had asked her to pass her the small tin box she'd found at the bottom of her underwear drawer and had opened it to reveal a dazzling starburst of sapphires and diamonds on a heavy gold chain.

'Your father gave it to me all those years ago, as

a token of his love, so it's very special. I want you to have it.'

'Is it real?' Rosie's face had felt so tight she'd barely been able to get the words out, and her mother's radiant, dewy-eyed smile had cancelled out her immediate and uncharitable thought that the glittering thing was just as much a tawdry sham as his love had been.

'It's very valuable, darling. So you must take great care of it. He told me it had been in his family for many years.'

Then you should have sold it, made life a bit easier for yourself—but Rosie had bitten the words back. She really couldn't be so cruel when the wretched 'love token'—or pay-off?—had meant so much to her mother.

Coming up against the dressing table, Rosie met her stormy eyes in the looking glass and vowed that if she ever got to meet her father she'd give the pendant right back to him. He could give it to his new wife, she thought furiously. She didn't want the hateful thing!

Screwing her eyes shut, Rosie took a deep breath and let it out slowly. The situation was really getting to her. She wasn't a vindictive person; on the contrary Jean had always maintained that she was too trusting and anxious to please for her own good. So she would stop thinking nasty thoughts about the man her mother had loved, the man she was in no position to judge, and get on with what she'd come here to do.

Though precisely what that was she had no clear idea. Coming face to face with her father had been her objective; in his absence all she could do was explore the house that his family had inhabited for many generations and hope, somehow, to pick up some clues to his personality.

There were four bedrooms and a bathroom on the attic floor. Sharon had grumbled. She didn't see why they should be stuffed up there when there were loads of unoccupied grand bedrooms on the first floor. She fancied living in luxury for once in her life. 'I only took this poxy job to get some cash for when I move into my boyfriend's pad in town. I've had it up to here with being stuck in this village—it's a one-horse dump!'

Privately, Rosie thought that the rooms they'd been given were lovely. Full of character, with their sloping ceilings, uneven plaster and dipping floors and pretty sprigged curtains at the windows set high beneath the eaves. And from the little she'd seen of the village it was lovely, too, and she was looking forward to Sunday, her day off, when she could explore and find the cottage where her grandparents had lived all their married lives and see where her mother had been born and raised.

But she'd kept her opinions to herself because—short though their acquaintance had been—she'd quickly learned that when Sharon grumbled she wasn't to be argued with.

Picking her way down to the first floor, she stood for a while listening to the silence. She had the house to herself.

Sharon's boyfriend had picked her up as soon as they'd finished supper. She'd been dressed in a purple mini skirt and a glittery black sweater, neither garment doing anything to disguise her bountiful lumpiness. Mrs Partridge, rising from the table to stack the dishwasher, had reminded her, 'I lock up at eleven and, no, you can't have a key, Sharon, so don't bother asking. If you're not back by then you'll be locked out.' To Rosie, when the other girl had swung out of the room with a defiant toss of her startlingly red curls, she'd added, 'Feel free to watch television and make yourself a hot drink if you want one. I'm off to my own quarters to put my feet up.'

And, in spite of the Spaniard's saying that he was here to oversee the mammoth spring cleaning exercise, Rosie hadn't clapped eyes on him since that encounter in his bedroom. From what she could gather, from Sharon's gossipy chattering and probing over the meals they'd shared with Mrs Partridge, Sebastian Garcia had had a call from the London head office of Troone and Garcia and had made a swift exit.

Which was just as well, Rosie thought, with a wry smile for the sheer immensity of her folly. He had just about knocked her for six at that initial, brief meeting and she wasn't here to embarrass herself by mooning over someone so completely unattainable and show herself up for the naive and foolish creature that she was by blushing and stammering whenever he was around.

So she had her father's unnervingly large, rambly and upper-crusty home to herself. It was the sort of place whose interiors she'd seen in the quality magazines she'd flicked through in the dentist's waiting room. Her legs beginning to shake because she was feeling like a sneak thief all over again, she turned her back on the narrow stairs that led down to the kitchen regions and headed for the main polished oak staircase.

Creeping down, she had to remind herself very sternly that she wasn't doing anything wrong. She had a right to be here—well, a sort of right, surely? And all she wanted to do was soak up the atmosphere and see if she could find out from the books he read, family photographs, maybe, what kind of man her father really was.

The main hall was lit by a solitary table lamp and the glow from the dying fire, and just as she set her feet on the massive flagstones a grandfather clock chimed the hour of eight from a dim and shadowy corner and made her jump out of her skin.

She'd been about to scurry back to her attic room, and her hand shot up to steady her bumping heart. It was the shape of the pendant beneath her T-shirt that gave her the courage to go on. To stiffen her spine and cross the floor to open doors and flick on lights. Large rooms led to much smaller, tucked-away ones, the furniture shrouded against the depredations of the departed and unlamented decorators.

At last, descending two worn stone steps, she thrust open an ancient door of highly polished broad oak planks and found herself in what had to be Marcus Troone's work room. Her eyes widened as she took in the book-lined study with its low, heavily beamed ceiling. It had been brought into the twenty-first century by the addition of a long custom-built desk which housed a computer system, fax machine, a bank of files and two telephones.

The book-filled shelves drew her. Beautifully bound classics—both ancient and modern—tomes devoted to viticulture, the poems of Wilfred Owen, masses of biographies, three yards worth of paperback whodunits and a whole tranche of gardening books. And, what she'd been looking for, right at the far end of one of the lower shelves: a bulky photograph album.

Her mouth going dry, Rosie carried it to the desk. Her hands shook as she opened it to a series of wedding photographs. Her father? A blond, craggily handsome young man with a beautiful dark-haired girl wearing a dream of a wedding dress, posing outside a small weathered stone church. Lots more—she flicked through the pages, met the smiling eyes of the dark-haired girl holding the reins of a pony, a small grinning boy on top. The same girl in a wheelchair, apparently directing operations while a middle-aged man was planting a tree. Could it be her grandfather? It was difficult to tell.

So far there were no more photographs of Marcus Troone: presumably he'd been behind the camera, she decided frustratedly. Until, right at the back of the album, a threesome standing in front of a huge greenhouse. Her grandfather, the stern features she remembered from her childhood relaxed and happy, her mother, a slender slip of a girl, clad in a checked shirt and old corduroy trousers, her blonde hair blowing in the breeze, her smile radiant. And Marcus Troone—her father—standing at her side, smiling down at the vitally lovely young Molly Lambert. Her mother.

Rosie felt sick.

Her mother had looked so happy back then. She would have had no idea what the future held for her on that long-ago summer's day.

Hands shaking, her heart thumping, she closed the album and carried it back to where she'd found it. But putting it back proved a problem. It just wouldn't go!

Biting her lip, she got down on her hands and knees and pulled out a book that seemed to be obstructing progress. That last photograph had really upset her; the album seemed to be burning her unsteady hands. She wanted rid of it.

She dropped it and could have screamed her head off when a few loose pictures fluttered to the floor. She shouldn't have touched the wretched thing. She wished she hadn't!

Passing through the hall, Sebastian paused to throw more logs on the dying fire. He was tired and hungry. The place felt deserted. Madge would have retired to her rooms. He guessed he could stretch to making himself an omelette and wind down in front of the fire with a glass of wine. Or two.

His tense features began to relax just a little. Driving back had been a nightmare of roadworks and clogged motorways. He should have spent the night in town and now he wondered why he hadn't. At least he'd sorted out the head office panic over a planning permission hiccup concerning the new hotel complex in Greenwich. And, barring more cries for help from a business manager who should have looked at things more logically instead of flapping, he should be able to get the Troone Manor show on the road.

Just one more chore—checking Marcus's fax machine—then he could fix himself something to eat.

Heading for his partner's study, he wondered how the new recruits were settling in.

Sharon Hodges had quite a reputation in the village. Bone idle and no better than she should be, so the gossips said. Grinning wryly to himself, he decided she was either lying on her bed eating chocolates or dyeing her hair a new and startling colour and trying to decide which of her current boyfriends was most likely to come up to scratch, whisk her away to the bright lights and keep her in the manner to which she would like to become accustomed.

And the other one, Rosie Lambert. Hadn't Madge mentioned that today was her birthday? Was she out celebrating with friends? A special boyfriend, maybe? From what he recalled from their brief meeting she was quite a looker. But vulnerable, too. Fragile.

The idea of some callow youth sniffing around her brought his brows down as he opened the door to his partner's study. Then he held his breath just before his scowl fled and was replaced by a grin that threatened to split his face.

'This is getting to be a habit.'

On her hands and knees, Rosie froze. She knew that voice. Her slender body was suffused with pleasure, it wriggled with sharply sweet sensations all over her. But, oh my goodness, what would he be thinking? That she had no business being in this room?

'I'm sorry.'

She had to grit her teeth and force herself to her feet, clutching at one of the loose photographs she'd been scrabbling around to retrieve. Her face felt hot and she felt such a fool, especially when he gave her that slow, sexy smile and said, 'Don't be.'

He could get used to opening doors to be met by the sight of that curvy little backside, clad tonight in shape-hugging worn denim!

He smiled into her anxious eyes, hiding a stab of annoyance. 'Surely you're not still working?'

What was Madge thinking of? Granted, there was a lot of hard physical graft to get through here, but making this delicate little creature work overtime was way out of order and he'd make damn sure it didn't happen again!

Butterflies were rampaging around in Rosie's stomach and she couldn't get her lungs to work properly. She'd tried to stop gawping at him but how could she when he was so gorgeous? The sharp grey business suit he was wearing did nothing to disguise the raw power of his magnificent physique and, try as she might, she couldn't help wondering what would happen if he kissed her.

She'd probably go into a terminal swoon, she thought in dire agitation and managed, finally, to give him the answer he was waiting for. 'No. I knocked off ages ago. I was looking for something to read,' she mumbled, uncomfortably aware that her face was bright scarlet. Lying to him made her feel horrible, but what choice did she have? She could hardly tell him the truth.

And she'd have to explain away the photograph she was holding. Bend the truth again. And the way those sultry, smoky eyes were pinned on her wasn't helping any. She felt as if she were drowning in wicked sensation. Her throat strangely tight, she croaked out, 'I was clumsy, I knocked that off the shelf—' she gestured jerkily to the album on the floor '—and photographs fell out.'

'No damage done.'

Sebastian's dark brows met. *Dio mio*—why was she so nervous? She looked like a puppy waiting to be beaten for some minor misdemeanour! Was she accustomed to being chastised for the slightest accident? A powerful surge of anger tightened the muscles of his shoulders. He'd like to meet the brute who had done that to her!

Madre di Dio!—her soft, full mouth was trembling now! He made a conscious effort to stop frowning—it was obviously giving her the jitters—relax his shoulders and approach her slowly.

'May I?'

Sebastian plucked the photograph from Rosie's suddenly nerveless fingers and his gentle, velvety tone made a wave of startling heat wash right through her. Her breath coming in short stabs, she tried to come to terms with the weird effect he had on her. It was a new phenomenon as far as she was concerned and one she could well do without, she decided grittily, as she felt her breasts lift beneath their thin cotton covering and crossed her arms over them to hide the embarrassing evidence.

His lips curved as he glanced at the image he held in his long fingers. 'This brings back memories—my aunt Lucia giving me my first riding lesson.'

Silvery eyes met hers, inviting her to share, and, desperately afraid that he would guess that she was helplessly attracted to him and laugh his socks off, she obliged and stared at the picture of the lovely young woman, the fat pony and the grinning little boy.

He would have been about six or seven, she thought moonily, then made herself snap out of it and tried to sound borderline intelligent as she hazarded, 'Your aunt was Sir Marcus's wife?'

'She was.' A flicker of sadness darkened those sultry eyes as he bent and slotted the loose photographs back in the album. 'Lucia was a truly beautiful person, both inside and out. But unlucky. Shortly after that snapshot was taken she was diagnosed with MS. It progressed rapidly. The unfairness of it used to make me angry. Still does, whenever I think about what her life became.'

Watching him replace the album in its original position, Rosie felt decidedly queasy. He would be absolutely furious if he ever discovered that his godfather and present business partner had betrayed the aunt he had so clearly idolised and that she, the humble cleaning lady, was the unfortunate by-product of that long ago affair!

She lowered her eyes in humiliation. She knew she ought to scrub her plans for making herself known to her father before any real damage was done, and yet part of her stubbornly yearned to find out if Sir Marcus really had loved her mother, to discover whether she could trust him or if she should despise him. She couldn't help wanting to be accepted, to have someone she could call family.

'You OK?' Sebastian swept her drooping figure with narrowing eyes. He held out the book she had obviously selected, leaving it leaning against the lower shelf when she'd dislodged the album. *British Military Swords* seemed a strange choice for such a scrap of a kid. 'You're very pale.'

'I'm fine,' she mumbled, mortified, clutching the book to her heaving breasts, hoping against hope that he hadn't noted the title and marvelled at her supposed choice of reading matter and wouldn't start to ask awkward questions, like how long had she been interested in the subject.

She looked far from 'fine', Sebastian decided. And she wasn't a scrap of a kid, either. She was twenty years old today, he remembered, and said warmly, 'Happy birthday, Rosie.'

The commonplace salutation evoked a response way out of proportion to its significance. But it had been worth it to see those drowning sapphire eyes dance as they met his, and her sudden radiant smile was so lovely it took his breath away.

'How did you know? No one else does.' It was the first birthday greeting she'd had all day, and coming from him it was very special, making up for the fact that she'd not had a card from Jean, who had never—ever since she'd been little and shopping at the mini-market with her mother and Jean had told her to choose from the exciting selection of sweets on offer—forgotten to mark the day.

'Madge happened to mention it,' Sebastian offered gruffly, his veiled eyes lingering on the flush of wild rose colour that deepened the clear deep blue of her fantastic eyes. In his experience, such genuine pleasure was a rarity in the female of the species. It would take more than a birthday greeting to get a reaction like that from the female sophisticates who moved in his circle—would take something in the order of a suite of diamond jewellery or a new car!

He felt strangely humble and not a little proprietorial as he commanded a touch thickly, 'Share a bottle of wine with me to mark the occasion.'

Now where had that come from? He was as surprised as Rosie looked. After the twenty-four hours of aggravation and frustration he'd just had he'd wanted nothing more than a simple meal and the chance to relax.

Her soft mouth had dropped open. She had to clamp it shut and clear her throat before she could say a single thing. She stared at his knock-'em-dead features, the taut bones beneath the smooth bronzed skin and gulped shakily, 'No, thanks. There's no need, honestly.'

The invitation had been the very last thing she'd expected and she knew he'd only asked because he felt sorry for her, the birthday girl with no party to go to.

He probably gave to every beggar he came across and rescued stray cats and dogs—and, as far as she was concerned, spending time with him, drinking wine with him, would be disastrous. She'd only go and give herself away and he'd end up knowing what up to now he couldn't even suspect—that she fancied him rotten!

If he'd wanted a let-out he'd been handed one on a plate. But, perversely, he wasn't going to take it. All traces of tiredness had fled. Obviously her birthday had gone unnoticed, Sebastian thought with a stab of annoyance. Remedying that would be his good deed for the day, he decided, finding he rather like the idea.

'You'd be doing me a favour, Rosie. The last twenty-four hours have been hectic. I want to unwind over a glass of wine and I don't care to drink alone.'

That had got her, he thought on a surge of satisfaction as he saw her brilliant eyes widen with sympathy, her delicate brows peak. Find the weak spot and go for it was a rule that worked well both in business and personal relationships. He knew little about Rosie Lambert, but his gut instincts told him she had a soft, sympathetic nature and would always answer a cry for help.

He pressed home his advantage. 'Please?'

That dark drawl, the honeyed Spanish accent, sent quivers of something fiery racing down her spine, making her gasp. She met the smoky sultriness of those black-fringed eyes and her mouth ran dry. At least his invitation hadn't sprung from pity, he was asking a favour, and that gave her the confidence to push out croakily, 'OK, if that's what you want.'

'Gracias.'

His smile made her head spin, and when he put a casual arm around her shoulders and led her from the room it was all she could do to stay upright. The touch of his hand through the thin fabric of her T-shirt scorched her skin right through to the bone and the heat of her body's instinctive and immediate response curled and tightened low down in her pelvis.

Get a grip! she snarled silently at herself as she sternly resisted the pressing temptation to sag against him, lay her head against that wide chest, slip a hand beneath that beautifully tailored jacket and feel the warmth of his body beneath the crisp fabric of his shirt.

So, OK, Sebastian Garcia was lethally attractive, and without even trying he could make things happen to her body that had never happened before, but he wouldn't look twice at the likes of her, she reasoned as he disappeared to fetch the promised wine after guiding her to one of the squashy sofas in front of the glowing hall fire.

She sat gingerly in one corner and tucked the book under a cushion out of sight. She'd have to replace it in the morning. Bedtime reading—as if! He must think she was pretty strange!

Dismissing it from her mind, she tried to relax. She'd drink one small glass of wine, toss a few aimless remarks in his direction and keep her eyes firmly fixed on anything other than him. Looking at all that masculine perfection would be her downfall. She would never survive the humiliation if he guessed she was hopelessly attracted to him.

He was taking much longer than she'd expected and with every minute Rosie got more uptight. Had he got sidetracked, forgotten all about her? Unlike him, she was easy to forget, she thought on a sickening surge of shame. She felt a real fool, sitting here like a lemon, and was about to slink off to bed when he re-entered the hall.

Her heart jumped and she forgot to breathe as he put two glasses and an opened wine bottle on a side table, then turned to her. In the dim light his smoky eyes mesmerised her. She could drown in those silvery depths, she thought helplessly, forgetting her earlier clear-headed decision not to look at him if at all possible.

Trouble was, her head was a total muddle when he was around.

He took something from the tray and walked towards her with the indolent grace that made her toes curl in her scuffed old plimsolls.

'For you.' Bending slightly from the waist, one of his hands uncurled her bunched together fist while the other deposited a single, perfect white camellia, slightly tinged with pale lemon colour at the ruffled centre, in the palm of her small hand.

A corner of his mouth curled wryly. 'I stole it from Marcus's greenhouse—though I'm sure he wouldn't mind. Not much of a birthday gift, *ciertamente*, but perhaps it will make you smile?'

Sebastian straightened abruptly. *Madre di Dio!* She would think he was shooting a line! The impulse that had sent him to cut that bloom now seemed ridiculous.

Until he had what he'd unconsciously known he'd been missing. That smile. And then he knew that the impulse hadn't been ridiculous at all.

Her eyes were on the blossom she held cupped in the curve of her hands, thick sweeping lashes hiding her expression, her silky blonde hair falling forward, a stray tendril kissing the petal-soft skin of her cheek. And then it began. A slight trembling of those luscious lips, an upward curve and then that radiant, brilliant smile her fathomless eyes winging towards his, deepest purest blue sparkling with dancing lights.

'It's perfect,' she breathed, and then, propelled by something far stronger than his formidable will, he bent towards her again, dipped his dark head, and kissed her.

CHAPTER THREE

ROSIE'S enticing lips were even softer and sweeter than he could have imagined they would be in his wildest dreams. Cool and still for that first split second—a challenge to his male ego. Then warm, warmer, exploding into an earth-shattering response.

As Sebastian's body leapt with a charge of forceful passion he felt an answering deep shudder of pleasure pulse through her slight frame and he placed his hands on her shoulders to steady her, or himself—he wasn't sure which—as a wave of atavistic male lust gripped and tightened every muscle in his own body.

As her lips parted, welcoming his entry, his kiss deepened and his mindless hands slid down to find her breasts. And *Dio mio!* they were so very beautiful. Small, pertly rounded, peaking nipples, blatantly aroused—perfect—

Her husky mew of drowning pleasure finally penetrated the red mist of lust that had fogged his brain. He went still, turned to stone as her sweet mouth clung, her small hands rising, fingers tangling in his hair, inviting, tormenting.

He dragged in a harsh breath. What in the name of all that was sacred did he think he was doing?

With a ragged inner groan for his own crass stupidity, he jerked upright, away from her, away from a deeper temptation than he had ever known, struggling to regain some semblance of his shattered self-control.

His heart crashing around against his ribs, he staunchly ignored the sudden, bewildered, lost look in her wide eyes, and turned away to hide the evidence of his aching sex.

'Wine,' he said, his voice roughened and raw. *Dio!* It had been a near disaster. A few more seconds and he'd have been making wild love to her right there on the sofa, and she would have been a push-over. Little Rosie Lambert deserved better than that!

His hand shook as he poured wine into two glasses. For the first time in his life he despised himself. It was a vile sensation! He'd been without a woman for so long he was turning into an animal!

Alcohol wasn't the best idea in the world, not in his inflamed state. But if he removed himself from her presence, as common sense dictated he should, she would know that what had happened back there had affected him catastrophically.

He had to act as though that kiss hadn't meant a thing to either of them. He wouldn't even apologise and suggest it was best forgotten. Just act as though it had been neither here nor there. Transmit the message that it had been just one of those things, not worth a mention.

Rosie was in shock. Her body was threatening to go up in flames. Sensations she hadn't known existed were bombarding her so that she didn't know whether she was on her head or her heels.

Why had he kissed her?

Why had he stopped?

Didn't he know that she hadn't wanted him to stop?

That kiss had been magic, heaven and excitingly scary all rolled into one and she'd wanted it to happen ever since she'd first clapped eyes on him! Didn't he know that?

Of course he did, the cool voice of rapidly returning sanity tartly informed her. He'd only meant to give her a brotherly birthday peck.

Because he'd been sorry for her?

And what had she done? Practically eaten him alive, begging for something he would never want to give! Then, to make matters even worse, his hands had sort of slipped down off her shoulders and come into contact with breasts that were still straining avidly against her top.

And while she'd gone all delirious, and so much out of her head she would have done anything he wanted her to do, he had jumped away just as if he'd had a very nasty shock and she'd never felt so humiliated and ridiculous in the whole of her life!

A solitary tear slipped down the side of her face and dripped on to the mangled petals of the camellia she'd scrunched up in an excess of sexual excitement. She scrubbed her damp cheek with the back of her hand and tried to smooth out the tattered blossom. She would probably press it and keep it for ever; she was daft enough, she thought despairingly.

Sebastian had turned. He held two glasses of wine. He looked as cool as a cucumber, she noted numbly. She couldn't bear it if he joked about her shameless behaviour or looked wary, as if he thought she was slightly insane and might jump on him and start tearing his clothes off!

But his gorgeous features were bland—just a small

polite smile playing around the sexy mouth that had so recently played havoc with every last one of her senses. He handed her a glass and took his own to the other end of the sofa and angled himself into the corner, his endless legs outstretched, casually crossed at the ankles, as far away from her as he could get without looking as if he were trying to avoid contact.

'You could have invited family or friends over this evening to help you celebrate your birthday, Rosie,' he remarked carefully, hoping his voice didn't give his dark thoughts away, give her the least intimation that he burned to kiss her again, run his hands through that tangled silky hair, explore every delicious inch of her lovely body, possess her.

He shifted uncomfortably, trying to blank the ache of sex from his mind and body, and said as levelly as he could manage, 'You're entitled to have visitors at any time when you're not working; I hope you know that. Neither Madge nor I would want you to feel imprisoned while you're working here.'

Relief shuddered through Rosie. Thank heavens he wasn't going to mention her awful behaviour. He was back in kind-employer mode and she couldn't regret that, not if she wanted to have some pride left.

So she cleared her throat and floundered for the cool part she knew she was expected to play. 'Thank you. But I don't have anyone to invite.' And could have bitten her tongue out when she saw his dark brows peak in what looked embarrassingly like sympathy. She had only been telling the truth, but how humiliating if he thought she was angling for his pity!

For something to do—something that didn't involve scurrying up to her room to hide her head under the pillow—she took a healthy gulp of the wine in her glass. It wasn't the cheap stuff, like the bottles she and Mum had shared on their birthdays because they couldn't afford anything halfway decent. It slipped down her throat like the softest of dark velvet.

Sebastian expelled his breath slowly. 'No one? Forgive me—Madge mentioned that you'd recently lost your mother—but what about your father, brothers, sisters?'

Skirting around the touchy subject of her father, Rosie said, 'No siblings. There was only ever Mum and me.' And took another long swallow of wine to disguise the sudden wobbling of her mouth.

Pretending to be cool and sophisticated was fine when it came to acting as if that kiss had been nothing special, merely the sort of thing that adults indulged in when there was nothing better to do. It was certainly salvaging her pride, but, my, was it difficult.

Leaning forward, his untouched glass of wine held loosely between his hands, Sebastian asked, 'What about your boyfriend?' and wondered why he had phrased the question so harshly. Why he'd phrased it at all, come to that.

It was none of his business but he'd bet his life on her having a string of them. Despite her ingenuous big blue eyes, the aura of vulnerability that had previously made his under-used protective genes work overtime, she was no novice when it came to sex. She'd been well and truly turned on a short while ago, more than willing.

He could have taken her just like that!

'I don't have a boyfriend.' Rosie lowered her eyes. His were glittering at her, as if she'd done something wrong. But he was only trying to make conversation and being nice about her having visitors. So why was she feeling so jumpy and on edge when it was patently obvious by now that he was being a gentleman and wasn't going to shame her by mentioning the way she'd kissed him as if she were a sex-mad trollop?

Meaning she was between men? Sebastian's mouth tightened. He wouldn't ask. It wasn't of the slightest importance. She was blushing again, he noted, her long thick lashes veiling her eyes, her full lips slightly parted. Kissable.

'You mean you haven't a man in your life at the moment?' He heard the words slip out and despaired of himself. Why couldn't he leave the subject alone? He was behaving totally out of character and didn't know why.

Rosie drained the last of her wine in sheer desperation. Why the inquisition? He was looking incredibly macho and domineering right now, his powerfully virile body really tense. And why didn't he just keep quiet and so give her the opportunity to say goodnight, thanks for the wine, and take herself off to her room?

He couldn't be interested in the state of her love life. Could he? No, of course not.

If this was a soppy romantic film he would be asking because he wanted to know if the coast was clear for him to start up a relationship with her. But real life wasn't like that and she wasn't daft enough to think it was. Wealthy, handsome, hard-headed businessmen didn't have relationships with nobodies.

Metaphorically planting her feet firmly back on the ground, she told herself that as he was standing in for her absent employer he would naturally want to vet her thoroughly.

A horrible thought struck her and made her feel physically ill. He had doubtlessly decided that, after her lustful earlier display, she made a habit of inviting all and sundry into her bed and he might have to face the distasteful experience of finding a string of rampaging males queuing up outside!

The ridiculous scenario made her feel hysterical. She pulled in a steadying breath. She could at least put his mind at rest on that score!

'I have never had a boyfriend.' Red flags of embarrassment flamed over her face. Girls at school had teased her mercilessly because, unlike them, she'd never had loads of boyfriends and experimented with sex. Her mother had vetoed out of school friendships with the rough crowd who lived on their estate. Besides, she hadn't been interested. She had the first-hand knowledge of what a casual fling had done to her mother.

Angry regret at that sorry fact tightened her voice as she scrambled to her feet and informed him, 'I left school to look after my mother. She was ill. Dying. Inoperable cancer. Towards the end she could have gone to a hospice, but she didn't want that. Neither did I. I nursed her. It didn't leave any time for socialising. So don't worry.' She huffed out a bitterly angry breath and put him straight. 'I'm not about to hang a red light outside Sir Marcus's front door!'

Placing her empty glass on the tray beside the half empty bottle with an angry little click, she bade Sebastian a cool goodnight and headed off up the stairs. She had never felt quite this assertive before in her entire life, or so cross. She placed her feet firmly on the treads and lifted her chin in the air. Right at this moment, she almost hated the gorgeous Sebastian Garcia!

In fact, when she really thought about it, she was damn sure she did!

Dismissed and firmly put in his place! Sebastian's mouth slanted wryly. Just like that!

A totally new experience and he rather liked the challenge it presented. Always provided he wanted to take it up, of course. Which he didn't. His eyes narrowed, he watched Rosie Lambert mount the broad staircase.

Never had a boyfriend? Did he really believe that? Initially, he'd been struck by her aura of naivety, his instinct to protect. He'd have believed anything she chose to tell him. But her shattering response when his lips had brushed hers, the immediate arousal of her body, had told him she'd been down that road many times before.

Not that he'd seen it that way, not to begin with. He'd been fuddled by lust himself and had felt a real heel for getting so close and intimate in the first place. Only when his mind had cleared had he recognised the signals she'd been sending out. He could have taken her there and then and she would have encouraged him.

A dewy-eyed innocent? With instinctive male appreciation he watched the sway of her seductively rounded bottom as she neared the top of the stairs, and thought not.

Definitely not.

A girl that lovely would have had males swarming round her since she reached puberty.

He drank his wine and did his best to relax back on the sofa. Lying, or not, what did it matter? He'd be back in Spain in a couple of weeks and Rosie would be out of his life. Not that she was actually in it, he reminded himself forcibly. She was simply a temporary member of staff. Different from the women he normally mixed with and therefore intriguing in an odd sort of way. And sexy with it.

Shooting to his feet, he gave himself a refill and shrugged out of his suit jacket, removed his tie and opened the top two buttons of his shirt. He felt strangely overheated.

He had to concentrate on what was really important, put Rosie Lambert right out of his mind. Opening Marcus's eyes to the type of woman Terrina really was before he brought her back to England as his future wife was his immediate priority. Once the greedy little gold-digger was here at Troone Manor, with her feet under the table, so to speak, and an engagement ring on her finger, there would be no getting rid of her. It was up to him to see that things didn't get that far.

Turning back to the sofa, wine glass in hand, he glimpsed a corner of the book Rosie must have stuffed underneath the cushion and swore softly. Just as he was getting her out of his head she had jumped right back in there again!

In her rush to pull him down a peg she had forgotten her bedtime reading matter. His brows peaking again at her strange choice, he came to a snap decision. He would take it up to her. She'd only been gone a few minutes, not long enough to already be in bed. It would give him the opportunity to hand it over with some polite pleasantry, letting her know there were no feelings—hard or otherwise—over the happenings of this evening and thereby close the chapter completely.

Rosie had had the quickest shower on record. She felt all churned up as she pattered barefooted back to her bedroom, tying the sash of her old cotton robe around her overheated body.

Her clothes were still in an untidy heap on the floor, just as she'd left them. She and Sharon had been expressly instructed to take their daily washing down to the laundry room every evening, where Mrs Partridge would deal with them first thing in the morning and avoid a backlog.

Rosie kicked them under the bed. She was venturing nowhere. She couldn't run the risk of bumping into Sebastian again. Not this evening. Not ever, if she could somehow avoid it.

Her hands trembling, she lifted the pendant from where she'd left it on the old-fashioned washstand that served as a dressing table. She had worn it, for safe-keeping, ever since her mother had given it to her. Now the idea of fastening it back on again after her shower and having it next to her skin was repellent to her.

It glittered at her, an uncomfortable reminder of how close she'd come to copying her mother's mistake, of making love with an unattainable man, going down a road that led to misery.

Grabbing a handful of tissues, she wrapped it and

thrust it to the back of a drawer, then leant against the top of the chest, her heart pounding.

It would have been so easy. If Sebastian had wanted to make love to her she wouldn't have been able to stop him. She wouldn't have wanted to. And, despite knowing she was being utterly stupid, her body still clamoured for him, her breasts swollen and sensitised, an insistent sweet and burning ache between her thighs.

Just reliving those fleeting minutes when his tongue had plundered her eagerly parted lips, his mouth as hot as sin, the long hands that had caressed, shaped and moulded her aching breasts, made her knees go weak and the blood in her veins turn to liquid fire.

Clamping her soft lips together, Rosie pushed herself upright. She had to stop fantasising, pull herself together. It had only been a kiss, for heaven's sake! It had meant absolutely nothing to him. In fact, she was at pains to point out to herself, when she'd responded the way she had, far from turning him on, he'd backed off in double quick time!

So why had a simple kiss made her lose the sense she'd been born with?

Because she was twenty years old and had never had a boyfriend and her hormones were telling her it was time for her to find a mate?

But that didn't gel with what had happened when she'd had her first real kiss, did it? Dwayne Evans had been the acknowledged school stud. All the girls had drooled over him. Blonde, clean cut and hunky, he had fallen in beside her as she'd walked home on a dark December afternoon in what had turned out to be her final year at school.

She hadn't minded chatting, but when he'd grabbed her and kissed her hard and furiously she'd felt nothing but outrage, when she'd known darn well that all the girls in her class would have been swooning.

He had towered over her, but even so the ferocity of her fists flailing into his stomach had knocked him off balance, and the way she'd disgustedly wiped the back of her hand over her mouth as she'd tried to get rid of the taste of him had been more than enough for him to tell his mates that Rosie Lambert was a frigid bitch and put her on the receiving end of horrible lewd comments.

So what was the difference? She'd had hormones back then, hadn't she? The way Sebastian Garcia made her feel was an enigma.

She had come to find out what she could about her father, but had discovered something else instead. The unwelcome knowledge that, like her poor mother, she could fall victim to lust.

Disgusted with herself, she turned to the mirror, grabbed the hairbrush and dragged it with vicious swipes through her hair. She was blinking back tears when she heard a brisk tapping on her bedroom door.

It would be Sharon, back before lock-out time, wanting to chew over the evening she'd spent with her boyfriend. Perhaps listening to the other girl's racy chatter would take her mind off her own dreadful evening.

Pinning a smile on a mouth that was reluctant to do anything but droop, Rosie opened the door and the smile trembled and vanished.

Sebastian. Her eyes widened and her lips parted. She knew she shouldn't be staring at him but she couldn't stop. His soft dark hair was rumpled, as if he'd been running his fingers through it; it made him look rakish and tormentingly dangerous. His suit jacket had gone and the fine white fabric of his shirt clung to wide rangy shoulders and his muscular torso and tucked into the narrow waistband of those perfectly cut trousers.

And he was holding that wretched book!

Saying nothing.

The silence was electric. His eyes slid down to her quivering mouth then back up to hold her gaze with a shimmering silver intensity.

She heard him drag in a breath, saw his broad chest expand, and the brush dropped from her nerveless fingers. She couldn't have retrieved it if her life had depended on it; she was glued to the spot. Her heartbeats had gone crazy, suffocating her.

'You forgot your book,' he intoned, his voice roughened. He stepped closer. *Dio!* Did she have any idea of what she was doing to him? That skimpy cotton robe did nothing to disguise the fact that she was naked beneath it. The sash was tightly cinched around her tiny waist, but there the modesty ended.

Her eager breasts were thrusting against the thin fabric, the opening revealing the fine dew of perspiration that beaded the enticing valley between. He imagined himself lapping the moisture away and tried to blank out the wicked mind picture, and didn't come near to succeeding.

This woman could arouse and tempt him as no other woman had done before, just by being there. She had no need of the calculated feminine wiles that he had become cynically immune to.

She just had to be there.

He should have left the book where he'd found it. He should have had more sense than to come to her room.

Time to get the hell out of it.

His heart racing, he gritted his teeth and wordlessly handed the book to her.

She stepped forward, reached for it, and he heard the whisper of fabric against her skin as their fingers touched. A shock wave of electric sensation coursed clear through him and the book fell to the floor.

A tiny moment of intensely sizzling silence, then they both bent for it at the same time. Both pulling in lung-searing breaths to shatter that spiked silence. Both reaching.

Her hair tumbled over her face, pale blonde tendrils curving round her slender throat, the edges of her robe parting. Mesmerised, his body hardening out of control, he gazed at the revealed curve of smooth thigh and reached out, long fingers clamping round her narrow wrist.

Pulling her upright, he hauled her against his fevered body, drinking in the clean soapy scent of her, the heat of her flesh through the flimsy robe. And dipped his head to kiss her.

Rosie felt as if she were burning alive. Her legs had no substance. She melted against him, the evidence of his arousal blowing her mind. Her helpless response was way beyond her ability to control, and as his tongue slid between her eagerly parted lips she no longer cared. If this was all she would ever know of total bliss, she would take it with both greedy hands and leave regrets for the cold light of dawn.

CHAPTER FOUR

ROSIE woke from a troubled sleep long before dawn. Gingerly, holding her breath until her lungs ached, she edged herself away from the tantalisingly sexy warmth of Sebastian's naked, lean and muscular length.

Her body ached in all sorts of previously unconsidered areas and every inch of her skin still burned fierily from his ravaging kisses, but that was as nothing beside the hurt in her heart.

Torrid images of his tormentingly erotic exploration of her far-too-eager body, his lips and hands sending her wild, her response shatteringly immediate and shamelessly wanton until, driven almost out of her mind with desperate excitement, she'd pleaded with near sobbing impatience, 'Love me—please love me!' now filled her tortured mind with gut-wrenching shame.

His body had curved over her, slick and hot, his voice ragged as he'd groaned, 'I want you—how I want you!' and angled himself into her with driven need. His sudden pause as she'd given a small but sharp cry of pain had made her move frantically against him, inviting him deeper, urging him on with moans of pleasure because he mustn't stop, not for anything. It was too late and the ecstasy she hadn't known was possible was so tantalisingly close.

Too late for him, too. His hands sliding beneath

her buttocks, his breathing ragged, he'd plunged deeper, erotically and exquisitely gentle, and Rosie had been swept away by transcending pleasure, oblivious to everything but the beautiful perfection of his loving, until her body had exploded with cataclysmic peaks of ecstasy that matched his shattering climax.

He had held her, she remembered, her throat tightening as she tried to find the courage to wake him and remind him that he should go back to his own room before anyone else woke.

Nothing had been said in that dizzying aftermath. He had simply held her, stroking her hair in the heavily charged darkness until she had drifted into sleep. An uneasy, restless sleep.

What on earth must he think of her? It was too awful to contemplate. She hardly knew him and yet she had welcomed him into her bed, behaved like a real slut!

She had begged him to love her, she remembered, but love hadn't come into it, of course it hadn't. He'd had sex with her because she must have unknowingly sent out all the right signals. Saying she was ready, wantonly eager and more than willing!

Which had been all too true, hadn't it? she thought in an agony of squirming regret. So she couldn't blame him, could she? Any red-blooded male would take what was handed to him on a plate.

She was more like her poor mother than she'd realised. Molly Lambert had made love with an unattainable man and had never stopped to consider the consequences, living only for the next time she could be with her secret lover. So perhaps her father hadn't been as much to blame for what had happened, after all. Maybe he just hadn't been strong enough to walk away from something so blatantly offered.

She shuddered, absorbing the terrible shock of that shaming revelation, and Sebastian said, making all her nerves jump, sounding fully awake when she'd imagined him in a deep and sated sleep, 'Cold, *cara?* Come, lie with me and I will warm you.'

Her face flaming with deep humiliation, Rosie pushed out tightly, 'I don't think so,' fighting hard against the tide of melting willingness that so recklessly flooded through her body.

She wanted a repeat performance more than anything else in the world and she didn't know what had got into her, she thought wretchedly, feeling a huge sob build up, threatening to escape and display all her rampaging emotions to a man whose only possible interest in her was her perceived sexual promiscuity.

'We need to talk. Nothing else, I give my word,' he guaranteed, his voice more heavily accented than she had ever heard it before as he eased her back against the pillows and drew the covers up, tucking them around her quivering shoulders.

Rosie devoutly wished she could disappear off the face of the earth. He was going to make her promise never to breathe a single word about what they'd done; she just knew he was. It stood to reason, didn't it?

He wouldn't want anyone to know that the wealthy, respected businessman with upper crust connections had slept with the humble cleaning lady!

And she couldn't stand her corner and come back with the information that she was the daughter of a knight of the realm. She couldn't mention that to anyone, not until she'd spoken to her father, and perhaps not even then, because he might not want to be reminded of past indiscretions, might tell her to get lost.

Besides, it would only make Sebastian hate her as the evidence of Marcus's betrayal of his much loved aunt. And she couldn't bear that.

Her toes curled beneath the covers, every muscle tightening in fight or flight mode as she waited for him to say something really awful.

Propped up on one elbow, he was looming over her and she turned her head away, her long hair spilling out against the pillows.

Dawn light was filtering into the little room and a glance at what she could see of his now quelling features told her that what he was about to say would be deadly serious and deeply unflattering from her viewpoint. She gritted her teeth. She would have to take it, get it over with, and learn a salutary lesson.

Above the rapid thundering of her heart she could hear his even breathing and wished she could be as composed as he so obviously was. When he said gently, 'I have to go soon. Madge rises early and I wouldn't want you to be compromised,' her soft mouth trembled and tears stung beneath her eyelids.

He was a real gentleman. He wasn't treating her like a whore or calling her nasty names, not even swearing her to secrecy for his pride's sake. He was actually thinking of her.

Long fingers stroked a wandering strand of hair away from her brow then curled around her jaw, turning her to face him, his voice low and very thickly accented now as he stated, 'You were a virgin. Rosie, I should regret what happened, apologise, but in all honesty I can't. You were so—' He paused, as if his aptitude for the English language had suddenly deserted him. His fingers slid from her jawbone and tracked gently down the side of her throat. 'Sensational.'

The intensity of his level silver gaze, the stark masculine beauty of his features, the touch of his hand against her skin, made her feel helplessly dizzy. He had said she was sensational. Was she really? He wouldn't lie about it, would he? Why should he?

She wanted to hold him, to wrap her arms around him and tell him how swollen her heart felt, swollen with so much love she could barely contain it. Already her breasts were peaking beneath the covers, the insistent liquid heat between her thighs tormenting her. But his next statement made her go cold all over.

'As this was your first time, I don't expect you're protected.'

Her mouth dropped open and her eyes felt as big as dinner plates. She hadn't given the matter of contraception any thought at all. Despite Jean's opinion that she was still wet behind the ears she disagreed and thought of herself as being sensible and capable, but in this one instance she'd been so blown away—

'Protection against pregnancy,' Sebastian elaborated with soft patience, as if he had mistaken what was probably the imbecilic look on her face for incomprehension.

Wordlessly, Rosie shook her head, too ashamed of her reckless behaviour to say a single word. And shivered with mortification at his tone of self-castigating regret when he admitted, 'Neither did I. It was utterly inexcusable.' He swung off the bed. 'You might be pregnant, Rosie. It is something we both have to think about.'

The rustle of fabric as he pulled on the clothes that had been rapidly discarded a few hours ago made her throat fill up with tears. And when he tautly reminded her, 'We need to discuss the situation more fully—in the meantime, promise me you won't worry about it,' before leaving the room, she had never felt so lonely in the whole of her life, not even in those first wretched weeks after her adored mother had died.

'Promise me you won't worry'! How could he say that? History could be repeating itself and she had probably messed up her life! How could she not worry?

A quick shower. A rapid change of clothes. Sebastian let himself out of the silent house and into the early spring dawn. A long, brisk walk should help him get his head straight, confirm the decisions that were already beginning to take shape.

Then, as he was used to doing, he would act on them.

'It's all right for some!' Sharon grumbled through a mouthful of sausage and egg. But the appreciative look in her heavily made-up eyes had Rosie laying down the single slice of toast which was all she'd said she could manage.

Glancing through the kitchen window in the direction of Sharon's gaze, she saw Sebastian approaching through the fields and her heart jumped up into her throat. He was so gorgeous, no wonder the other girl was staring. Jeans and a chunky sweater only served to emphasise his powerful physique and his stride, in those walking boots, looked really purposeful.

Her stomach performed an alarming series of acrobatics. Ever since she'd steeled herself to present herself for breakfast her stomach had been misbehaving. Nauseous at one moment, as if she were already suffering from morning sickness, squirming with electrical charges at the memory of last night in the very next second.

'You've got to admit it, he's a real hunk,' Sharon pronounced, reaching for the toast and marmalade.

Madge said prosaically, 'The *Señor* will be hungry,' and stood up from the table.

And I might be pregnant, Rosie thought, and wondered why the idea didn't seem quite so alarming as it had done, then felt her face drain of colour as a horrible premonition crept into her mind. If history was going to repeat itself exactly then—'Is he married?' she heard herself blurting, although framing that question out loud hadn't been her intention.

Putting bacon and tomatoes ready for the grill, Madge gave a wry chuckle. 'Not that one! Once, when I told him it was time he settled down, he asked me why he should be satisfied with one flower when he could have a whole bunch. Still, I dare say the time will come.'

'Fancy your chances?' Sharon settled back in her chair and grinned unrepentantly. 'Forget it. If I thought there was any chance he'd go for one of the common herd I'd be in there, strutting my stuff! When he does marry, she'll have to be drop-dead fantastic, with a pedigree going back to the Ark and a sackful of dosh. His type wouldn't settle for anything less.'

As if she needed reminding! Rosie made her excuses and fled.

Sebastian entered the house via the service area, shed his walking boots and pushed his feet into an old pair of loafers. His timing was spot on: breakfast was in progress, he could smell grilling bacon from here. But when he walked through into the kitchen the stab of disappointment that speared through his entire body was so out of character that he feared for his sanity.

No sign of Rosie. Just a plate with a crumbled piece of toast where she must have been sitting, Madge making fresh coffee, Sharon reaching for the last slice in the rack, the seams of her brown overall straining.

Even in her over-large overall Rosie managed to look both endearing and nerve-tinglingly sexy, he recalled, as his common sense finally overrode his disappointment at not finding her here. The announcement he'd intended to make was burning his tongue but it could wait until they all met up for lunch.

'Jump to it, Sharon,' Madge ordered as she turned back to the table, cafetière in one hand, a fresh rack of toast in the other. 'Rosie's already hard at it. And I don't want to come up and find you gossiping and wasting time.'

Sebastian suppressed a grin as Sharon rolled her eyes and reluctantly hauled herself to her feet. Her jaw was set at a pugnacious angle as she stated, 'I'll work this week out, then I'm jacking it in. It's boring, and I ain't used to being treated like a kid. My boyfriend wanted to go clubbing last night, only we couldn't. He said to get locked out, see if I cared, I could stay over at his. He said to give you the elbow. But I told him I wouldn't get paid if I didn't work the week out, and I ain't scrubbing floors for nothing. Not for no one.'

She turned her angry reddened face to Sebastian, as if, he thought, as he poured his coffee, she was looking for his support. But her departure at the end of the week suited his plans just perfectly. He needn't make that semi-formal announcement after all.

He said smoothly, 'We'll be sorry to lose you, Sharon. Your mind's obviously made up so I won't ask you to change it.' And waited for her to stump out of the room before giving his attention to Madge. Who was fuming.

'That girl's as unreliable as the rest of her family! Now what are we going to do? Sir Marcus expects the house to be sparkling for when he brings that—his fiancée here. Rosie's a good worker but she can't do it on her own, not even with what help I'll be able to give her. And it's too late to go advertising again.'

'Relax, Madge. Sit down, won't you?' He waved her to a chair on the opposite side of the table and began to eat his bacon, surprised at his keen appetite after the demons of remorse and self-loathing that had been his companion in the early hours of the morning.

But he'd faced those demons, faced the possible repercussions of those heady hours when he'd slaked his lust on Rosie's tormentingly responsive, gorgeous body. It had been a reprehensible mistake on his part and the excuse that he had completely and quite uncharacteristically lost his head was no excuse at all.

But at least he now knew what he had to do.

Looking into his old friend's face, he said, 'Leave everything to me.' And he carefully spelled out the decisions he'd reached during his early-morning walk, too intent on enjoying his breakfast to note the way Madge's brows rose to her hairline as he spelled out his plans for Rosie.

Half an hour later he exited Marcus's study, the first part of his plan put into operation. A team of professional cleaners, based in nearby Ludlow, would be arriving first thing in the morning.

Now all he had to do was inform Rosie of the domestic alterations. She might dig her heels in, but hell, he thrived on challenges, didn't he?

His pace determined, he mounted the stairs quickly, heading for whichever of the rooms the girls were working in, alerted by Sharon's raucous laughter as he approached the master suite.

The door was open. He heard Sharon say, obviously in answer to a question Rosie had posed, 'Briar Cottage? 'Course I know it. Everyone knows everyone in this one-eyed dump. It's an estate cottage; the head gardener lives there. Why do you ask? Someone you know?'

'No, not really.' Rosie's voice was muffled, sounding slightly breathless. 'Someone who knew I was coming to work in the vicinity just happened to mention it. Said it was a picture. I just wondered where it was.'

'Turn right at the bottom of the drive, down the lane, first right again on to a track and you're there. It's OK, I suppose, if you like thatch and roses round the door stuff. Me, I'd rather go take a look at the inside of the travelling library—and that's saying something, believe me!'

Sebastian grinned to himself. Sharon obviously had no time for the delights of rural life. He walked through the doorway. Sharon was lying back on Sir Marcus's dust-sheeted bed, idly examining her bitten fingernails. She shot him a sullen look and shuffled off the bed, but Sebastian had eyes only for Rosie.

She had her back to him and was painstakingly cleaning the daunting expanse of the main small-paned window, the morning sunlight giving her beautiful hair shimmering silver highlights. Unlike the lazy Sharon, Rosie was putting her heart and soul into her work, intent on earning every penny of her wages.

A swamping wave of tenderness drenched through him, taking him by surprise. Whatever happened, he vowed, he wouldn't allow her to suffer for what had happened between them last night. It had been magical, instinctive, transcending his previous, admittedly slightly cynical experiences with the opposite sex. But he wasn't going to think about that, he told himself harshly, as he watched her stretch to reach a high corner.

He would wipe it from his memory banks and make sure it never happened again.

Oblivious of his silent appearance in the room, Rosie, rubbing at a stubborn smear, addressed her work-mate, 'I don't suppose you remember the family who lived in Briar Cottage before the present head gardener?'

'I do,' Sebastian slotted in, and watched her go very still, as if his voice had given her a huge shock, and added easily, his eyes on Rosie's now rigid shoulders, willing her to turn and face him, 'There's been a change of plan, ladies.'

Reluctantly, he turned to Sharon, who was now on her hands and knees, unenthusiastically dabbing polish on the oak boards. If anyone should be stiff with embarrassment it should be she, not Rosie, who had been diligently working. Unless she thought that idle chit-chat was forbidden.

If her questions had been idle?

Shelving that for the moment, he elaborated, 'I've decided to hire a team of professional cleaners. They start tomorrow. You'll be paid until the end of the week so you might as well pack your bags and leave now.'

Rosie's knees threatened to give way beneath her and she felt the colour drain out of her face. Despite telling her not to worry about possible repercussions following last night's frenzied lovemaking, he was giving her her marching orders! Getting rid of her in case there were consequences he wouldn't want to handle! So much for him telling her they had to get together and talk things out!

Besides, to add insult to injury, she'd only been here a few days and had found out next to nothing about her father, and found out too much about herself!

She hadn't even had the opportunity to look at the cottage where her mother had lived for the first eighteen years of her life.

But there was nothing she could do about it. She hadn't signed a contract or anything. She gathered up her cleaning materials and turned to watch as

Sebastian peeled notes off a roll and handed them to Sharon.

Determined that he wouldn't have the faintest idea how much she was hurting, she held her chin high as she watched him watch Sharon make a hasty exit. She knew the other girl had told him and Madge that she was leaving at the end of the week. So Sebastian had grabbed the opportunity to get rid of her as well. Like her mother before her, she had a lousy taste in men! And she wasn't going to cry—no way was she going to cry!

And he could keep his rotten money! She would accept only what was due to her for the few days she'd actually worked here. Her voice stiff and sharp, her chin still painfully high, she announced, 'I'll be ready to leave in ten minutes. And I'd like permission to use the phone to call a cab to get me to the station.'

He turned slowly, glittering silver eyes resting on her, his beautiful mouth softly curved as if her independent stand had amused him. Her breath snagging in her throat, Rosie turned her head away; if she looked at him she would disgrace herself and start to cry. Like her mother before her, she had fallen instantly and recklessly in love with the one man she should have run a mile from.

'You're going nowhere,' he stated, with such flat determination he aroused everything stubborn within her. 'I let Sharon go because the work didn't suit her. You're different.'

Because she believed in working for her wages? Because she didn't skive off and grumble about everything? A case of knowing a bargain when he saw one? It shouldn't hurt. But it did.

Moments ago she'd been on the verge of tears because she thought he was throwing her out. Suddenly everything had changed. She had fallen headlong into the mire of loving him, but she could get herself out of it, couldn't she?

She could cut her losses as far as meeting her father and getting to know him was concerned—he wouldn't be interested in any case. And rescue herself from the awful fate of falling even more deeply for Sebastian Garcia, falling so deeply that she would be spoiled for ever—unable to form a special relationship with any other man—just as her mother had been.

Her eyes very blue, she turned to him and made herself look into his strong, lean face. 'You don't need me. Professional cleaners will go through this place like a dose of salts. I'd just get in the way. I'd rather go.'

Even as she stated her intentions, as firmly as she was able, she felt desperately empty, as if she were suffering a loss beyond bearing. But it was the best way, the only way. Staying around would make her act like a real fool. Watching for him, hoping and praying for a kind word, a smile, lying awake at night longing for him to come to her room.

'Forget the cleaning,' he dismissed, clearly losing patience with her, his skin taut over his beautiful bone structure. 'I may have made you pregnant, remember?' he jolted acidly. 'I want you where I can see you until we're sure, either way. I took advantage of you, which in the cold light of day I deeply regret,' he admitted, mortifying her. 'However, I take my responsibilities seriously. You stay.'

What did that mean? Rosie questioned hysterically.

That if the worst happened he would book her into a private clinic and pay for an abortion? Well, he could forget that, for starters!

Her legs turning to jelly, she stared at the floor and mumbled, 'I can look out for myself.'

And shuddered uncontrollably as he took two swift paces forward, tipped her chin with an inescapable forefinger and ground out, as if he wished he'd never set eyes on her, 'No, you can't. And even if you could I wouldn't let you. I feel guilty enough as it is. Now.' He dragged in a tight breath and said more levelly, which must have called for a huge effort, Rosie decided miserably, 'Get changed. I'm taking you out for lunch. And while we're eating I'll tell you what I have in mind.'

As she opened her mouth to say thanks, but no thanks, he denied her the opportunity by putting both hands on her shoulders and giving her the benefit of his dazzling grin, 'Humour me, Rosie. Please?'

She could drown in that smile, in the depths of those glittering silver eyes. That unfair charisma coupled with the warm male scent of him made her tummy flip. Wordlessly, she nodded then dipped her head, hiding her suddenly wildly coloured cheeks. In this mood she could deny him nothing.

She was a hopeless case where he was concerned, and there didn't seem to be a blind thing she could do about it!

CHAPTER FIVE

GET changed! Into what?

Rosie swallowed hard on a huge surge of panic. Most of her gear was back in the room Jean had rented out to her above the mini-market. And, to be brutally honest, they weren't the sort of clothes women who lunched with Sebastian Garcia would be seen dead in!

She and Mum had been dressed by charity shops. You could pick up some real bargains. That they didn't always fit as well as they might, and the colours and fabrics were not what they would have chosen if money had been no object, was neither here nor there when being warm and decently covered on a shoe-string was the name of the game.

But what did it matter? she asked herself glumly as she pulled a pair of well-washed, worn old jeans out of a drawer. He wouldn't expect her to look like a fashion plate and he wouldn't be taking her to any-where posh.

Come to think of it, he shouldn't be taking her anywhere at all. He could easily have told her what his so-called plans for her were right there and then. And if she had any sense she would have firmly but politely vetoed them, whatever they were.

She could look out for herself without him telling her what to do and when to do it. She should have stood her ground, not weakly given in when he'd said please and made her go spineless and melty.

Pulling on a clean but faded turquoise sweatshirt, she wrinkled her nose at her reflection. Her first date with the kind of man who would normally be seen with a stunning, seriously loaded and beautifully dressed sophisticate on his arm, and she was dressed as if she were about to go out and dig the garden!

But it wasn't a real date, she impressed upon herself heavily. He was just worried about the possibility of pregnancy and was probably afraid that she'd publicly name him as the father, and he'd hate that, wouldn't he? He wouldn't want his fancy friends to know that he'd been sharing the cleaning lady's bed.

Feeling low and no-account, Rosie brushed her hair until it shone like silk, painted her mouth a vivid scarlet to make herself feel better and decided that if he was going to insist she stick around like a spare part until they knew one way or another, she could always fib. She didn't like the idea of lying to anyone, but surely, in this situation, it could be forgiven.

Her period wasn't due for another two weeks, but he wasn't to know that. So, in a couple of days, say, she could tell him he was off the hook, to his huge relief, and take herself off.

She couldn't bear the thought of having him constantly watching her, his regret for what had been so beautiful growing deeper by the day, the tension between them spiralling, spoiling her memories of what they had shared. She would rather get over her love for him in her own way, in her own time.

She exchanged her old plimsolls for a fairly respectable pair of brown lace-ups and was as ready as she'd ever be, and presented a fairly composed façade as he ushered her into the passenger seat of his opulent silver Mercedes. She tried to ignore the fact that he was dressed in a classic black cashmere sweater over superbly cut stone-coloured pants and looked seriously well-heeled and impossibly spectacular.

Composure was the name of the game, she lectured herself. They were bound to argue over what he had termed his plans for her—as if she had the mental ability of a gnat! So she had to stay calm and very controlled if she were to have any chance of impressing her rights over her own body on him.

But the cool veneer of composure cracked and blistered when, after a few wordless minutes, he brought the car to a halt on a narrow lane outside a small cottage.

'You wanted to see the head gardener's cottage,' Sebastian announced quietly, turning in his seat, one arm stretching over the back of hers, his silvery eyes so intent she gave an involuntary shudder. 'Any particular reason? It's an ordinary estate cottage and not on any tourist map that I know of.'

Her throat thickening with tears, Rosie pressed her soft lips together and turned her head away quickly, not wanting him to see how affected she was.

From the way he had parked she couldn't get a good look at Briar Cottage without looking round that handsome head, the expanse of black-clad shoulders.

Fumbling fingers released her seat belt and found the door catch. Rosie slid out of the car, willing her legs to keep her upright as she gazed at her mother's birthplace, an ache in the region of her heart.

A steeply pitched thatched roof topped a sturdy

timber frame. There were bright curtains at the small windows, a plume of smoke from the chimney and searing yellow daffodils and paler, subtler primroses growing amongst the cabbages.

A swing hung from an ancient pear tree. Had it been there when her mother was a child? Had she swung amidst the flowers and vegetables dreaming of her future? Dreams that had turned into what had to have been a nightmare of drudgery, of alienation from her parents.

'If you'd like to see inside I'm sure Mrs Potts wouldn't object.'

Rosie tensed. She hadn't heard him exit the car; she'd been listening to her memories. Her mother telling her that Gran had passed away a scant year after the death of her grandfather, and later, her lovely face white with strain, explaining that following the sale of the furniture and effects—everything arranged by the estate manager and a solicitor—the proceeds, according to her Will, were to go to charity.

'No.' She vetoed his suggestion, her voice thin and lifeless. The ache in her heart had spread all over her body as the enormity of what Marcus Troone had done to her mother punched home with a vengeance.

'You were asking Sharon if she recalled the previous head gardener. And I told you I did, remember?' Sebastian prodded gently, making the connection. 'I remember Joe Lambert from childhood holidays spent with Marcus and my aunt. You were related?'

Rosie shivered. There was little warmth in the early March sunshine and the light breeze was cutting. And there was no point in lying about this. 'They were my grandparents.' Her mouth felt numb. She could barely get the words out. 'I was—was just interested to see where they'd lived.'

'You never visited them.' That seemed pretty obvious. But odd. Sebastian's brows tugged down. Where he came from families meant everything.

She shook her head. The wind had blown a heavy strand of hair over her eyes, blinding her. Her hand shook as she brushed it away.

'You never met them?' He could scarcely believe it. His own grandparents, all now sadly missed, had treated him like a prince. A glance at her pale, anguished face turned his heart to treacle. He slipped an arm around her shoulders and pulled her slight body close. She was shivering. She was cold.

With an effort, Rosie pulled herself together. She had to, double-quick. The way he was holding her was testing her will-power to the limit. She so wanted to curve her body into his warmth, wrap her arms around him, cling to the wonderful male strength of him and unburden herself, tell him everything.

She mustn't. It would be a really stupid thing to do. He'd hurt her horribly when he'd said how much he regretted making love to her. She wouldn't be able to take it if she tried to get closer and he pushed her away, believing she was asking for much more than his comfort.

'Twice,' she mumbled. Then amended, 'They visited Mum after I was born, so I don't remember that time. Then came again when I was ten.'

Stiff, awkward, disapproving, both of them. They'd hardly said two words to her and the atmosphere had been really spiky. Her mother had shot into the bathroom when they'd gone and she'd heard her muffled sobs. But when she'd emerged five minutes later she had smiled, even though her eyes had been red and puffy, and had cheerfully suggested a rare treat, a visit to the cinema where the latest cartoon film was showing, such an exciting event that the incident had been forgotten.

'You're cold,' Sebastian said briskly. 'Let's go. The Bull in the village always has a good fire, and a passable menu.' He had intended to take her further afield, somewhere more special than the local pub. But the poor little scrap was obviously deeply upset and he wanted nothing more than to get her warm and relaxed as quickly as possible.

He wasn't stupid, he told himself as he started the engine and reversed back along the narrow track. He could put two and two together as well as the next man.

There had just been her and her mother. No mention of a father. It was obvious that her mother had been a single parent, and presumably Rosie's grandparents had disapproved to such an extent that they hadn't had their only grandchild over for holidays in the fresh country air, had probably told their daughter never to darken their doorstep, had virtually washed their hands of the pair of them.

Anger punched at his heart. He couldn't trust himself to speak until he'd got it under control. Had her father been one of the local lads? Had he done a runner when he'd learned that his girlfriend was pregnant, unable or unwilling to face the prospect of fatherhood?

He couldn't understand how a man could do that

and still live with himself! His stomach clenched. *Madre di Dio*—if he'd carelessly fathered a child on Rosie he would damned well do his duty! He'd be around for his child, make sure neither of them wanted for anything.

Had he ever seen Rosie's mother? He must have done. He tried to remember. The summer holidays spent with Marcus and his aunt, sometimes with his parents, sometimes staying on his own, had been too full of adventures—fishing, riding, building tree-houses and generally getting into mischief—to leave much time for noticing the estate workers' families.

But he had known that Joe Lambert had a daughter. She'd even helped her father in the gardens one summer, he recalled now.

Aware that his silence was doing nothing to make Rosie feel more comfortable, he broke it. 'Did you take the temporary job at the Manor because you wanted to see where your mother had grown up?'

'Partly,' Rosie admitted. She wouldn't tell him the rest of it; she couldn't. All he'd ever felt for her was a lust he now hated himself for, so it wouldn't make any difference to her if he ended up despising her for who she was. But she didn't want him hating her poor mother for being the woman Marcus had betrayed his adored aunt with.

'And after—after your mother left the village—where did she go? Where did you live?' He felt strangely driven to probe. 'From what I can gather, her parents gave her precious little support. How did she manage?'

The thought of anyone turfing a pregnant daughter out to fend for herself was utterly abhorrent to him.

And in this case it felt almost personal, he admitted, the depth of his feelings surprising him into shooting her a hard, level look.

Rosie wriggled in her seat, her stomach churning. He sounded so harsh. Really disapproving. And that look—the condemning silver eyes above those hard cheekbones—had flayed her. Of course, in the wealthy, rarefied atmosphere he inhabited single mothers living a hand-to-mouth existence didn't exist. If a rich and pampered member of his exalted circle made the mistake of getting pregnant she would be discreetly married off.

Sebastian Garcia might be wealthy beyond avarice, the intelligent driving force behind a highly successful business empire, but he knew nothing about the real world. When had he ever wondered where his next meal was coming from, or drudged all day for a pittance, or dressed in someone else's cast-off clothing?

Memories of her mother's tired, pale features, her unfailingly cheerful smile, floated into her mind. No one would belittle her, no one!

Staring ahead at the unwinding country lane, she said proudly, 'Mum was tough and so was I. The way we lived would probably have killed the likes of you! We had a council flat and we made it nice, despite the surroundings—the graffiti-spattered walls, the broken lifts and stinking stair-wells.

'Mum worked hard cleaning offices, and as soon as I was old enough I worked early evenings and Saturdays at Jean's corner shop. We managed on our own without the benefit of tiaras, fancy clothes, flash cars and servants to shield us from the contaminations of daily life!'

She almost added a childish 'so there' but stopped herself in time and stuck her lower lip out mutinously as they drew up in front of an ivy-clad pub on the outskirts of the village.

Exiting the car and skirting the bonnet, Sebastian hid a grin. In spite of her aura of fragile vulnerability, Rosie Lambert had mountains of spirit when it came to something she really cared about. He liked that.

He wanted to tell her to be proud of her mother, of herself, but thought better of it. She would only accuse him of patronising her.

He wanted to tell her that there were things great wealth could never buy: love and loyalty, for instance. But she obviously already knew that.

So he kept his mouth shut.

She was sitting in the car as if permanently welded to the seat, her arms crossed over her slender midriff. The grin threatened again. Suppressing it, he opened the door. She didn't bat an eyelid. She didn't need to say she didn't want to be here, didn't want to have lunch with him. Her body language said it for her.

Leaning forward, he reached in to undo her seat belt, since she obviously had no intention of doing it for herself. The back of his hand brushed the soft, sweet undercurve of her breast and his heart raced with carnal sensation. *Infierno!* What she did to him!

He stood back quickly, outraged at his body's treachery. He had made one unforgivable mistake. He wasn't going to repeat it.

'Hurry,' he ordered briskly. 'Before the heavens open.' Black clouds had raced in, heavily obliterating the earlier clear blue skies, and the wind had risen, a precursor of the storm to come.

Averting his eyes, he waited while she edged reluctantly out of her seat and stood beside him. The top of her silky gold head barely reached his shoulders. Her hair smelled of fresh air and flowers.

He brutally slapped down the temptation to bury his mouth in it and turned abruptly, striding over the forecourt, past the wooden seats and tables that flanked the open door. He waited, his hands bunched into his trouser pockets while she caught up with him, then, nodding towards the bar where an open fire burned brightly in the brick inglenook, strode to too-brusquely request coffee and a menu from the landlord.

Selecting a round table nearest the fire, Rosie held her hands out to the welcoming blaze and forced herself to relax. The cold was gradually seeping out of her veins. Sebastian was talking to the man behind the bar. How gorgeous he was. She could hardly believe she was here at his invitation, especially after all his retrospective disgust at the way they'd both behaved. Had Sir Marcus brought her mother here? Given her lunch? No, of course not. He'd been a married man and would have insisted that their meetings were a dark secret.

Not wanting to lumber herself with all that anger again—she had stopped being annoyed with Sebastian at last because it wasn't his fault he'd been born with a drawerful of silver spoons in his mouth—she pondered happier things. Like, had her mother sat with her friends on those benches outside on warm summer evenings, chatting and laughing, drinking fizzy pop out of bottles, eating crisps and talking about hairstyles, teachers, exams and pop stars?

She liked to think so, to believe that for the first eighteen years of her life—until the fateful day when she'd fallen in love with Marcus Troone—her mother had been happy and carefree—

'Warmer now?' Sebastian pulled out a chair and sat opposite her, laying down the typed menu, pushing aside the ashtray and the broken-handled mug that held half a dozen daffodils. Her eyes were sparkling, her pale cheeks brushed with tender colour. He stared at her, his silvered gaze intense between narrowed lids. His heart kicked. She was beautiful. Dress her in decent gear and she'd be an absolute stunner.

He swallowed. Hard. Having her with him where he could keep an eye on her, make sure she didn't simply disappear taking his maybe-child with her, was the only viable option, but it was going to be difficult. Keeping his hands off her would be the main stumbling block.

He thrust the menu at her. 'Choose what you'd like to eat,' he said brusquely, and saw the immediate stubborn set of her lovely mouth, the way she set the typed sheet aside without even glancing at it, and silently cursed himself. He was handling himself badly; he knew that. He had never been in this situation before. He had never met a woman who could make him behave like a reckless, callow youth, ruled by his hormones.

He'd never had unprotected sex before, run the risk of an unwanted pregnancy. But was it unwanted? The thought of her beautiful body blossoming and ripening for him, of holding their child in his arms, made everything inside him melt, his brain turn to fog.

Infierno! What was happening to him?

The arrival of their coffee came as a relief. He ordered cottage pie for both of them as it appeared to be the only home-made item on offer, decided against wine, and got himself firmly back on track. The mover and shaker. The man in control.

'Do you have a passport?' he asked with studied politeness and not a great deal of hope, and struggled not to applaud her spirit when she came back proudly.

'Of course I have. Why wouldn't I? Don't domestic skivvies travel abroad where you come from?'

'Frequently.' Hiding a grin, he relaxed back in his chair, admiring the cool blue challenge in her fantastic eyes, the haughty angle of her delicately pointed chin. 'So tell me about your travels.'

Rosie huffed in a breath. Just because she'd gone and fallen in love with him that didn't mean she had to take umbrage whenever she decided he was acting all superior! Let's face it, he was superior to her in every way there was, she decided gloomily, and woodenly supplied, 'Paris. On a school trip.'

She hadn't told her mother the excursion was being arranged. She had known there was no way it could be afforded. But the school secretary had written to the parents of all the pupils in her class and Mum, of course, had stated that she wasn't to be left out. And had taken on an extra office cleaning contract. Her eyes misted and she could feel the all-too-familiar lump in her throat, and she couldn't speak when Sebastian asked softly, 'Didn't you enjoy it?'

Something had deeply saddened her. He hated to

see it. Unlike most of the women he knew she was unable to hide her emotions. Radiant happiness at something as simple as a birthday greeting that had cost nothing to say or the gift of a purloined flower, carelessly given, raw grief over something unknown to him.

Catching the mute misery in those brilliant sapphire eyes, he vowed that in the coming weeks he would know every single thing about her. It was important.

As important as knowing that she had been capable of total, honest generosity when she had made him the gift of her body, openly revelling in the driven, selfish needs of his hands, his lips—Blank that! Right now!

He cleared his throat sharply. He had to move this forward. And watched with deep compassion as she struggled for composure as their meal was put on the table.

As soon as they were alone again he stated levelly, 'If you're wondering why I asked, I have to return to Spain. I was planning to, in ten days or so. But now that the domestic arrangements at Troone have altered I'll be bringing the date of my return forward. I want you to come with me.'

A beat of total, shocked silence, then, 'I couldn't do that!' Rosie reddened. Why would he want her to? It didn't make any sense, unless—her heartbeats went haywire—unless he'd changed his mind about having sex with her again. The possibility was endlessly exhilarating but she had to resist the wicked temptation. A secret and definitely short-lived affair would damage her more than she already was!

'You don't have any option.' Sebastian was right

back in control, where he should have been all along. 'I have to be in Spain so you do, too. I might have made you pregnant, in case you'd forgotten,' he tacked on drily, tasting the cottage pie, which was surprisingly good. 'I need to be sure, one way or the other. I'm not a man to duck out of my responsibilities. I need you where I can see you. I don't want you panicking and disappearing.'

Rosie wanted to fall through a hole in the floor and never be seen again. She put down the fork she had only just picked up before it dropped from her nerveless fingers. True, unlike her father, he took his responsibilities seriously. But did he have to be so matter-of-fact and deadpan about it? She felt deeply humiliated, a real nuisance. And what had she been thinking of? That he was suddenly finding the idea of having sex with her again utterly irresistible?

As if!

'Think of it as an expenses-paid holiday,' he stated, supremely sure of himself—and thankfully unaware of what was churning round in her mind, Rosie thought, wondering how he could be so cool about a situation which was anything but.

His gorgeous features might have been carved from stone for all the emotion they displayed. It would be easier if he told her she was a pain in the neck and blamed the whole mess on her. At least she could then have a stab at hating him, instead of fancying him rotten and praying for a miracle that would make him fall in love with her.

Whatever he said in that detached, authoritative voice of his, no way would she go to Spain with him, demean herself by being dragged around like an unwanted piece of luggage that had to be watched over in case it turned into a time bomb!

She could always excuse herself, right this minute, go to the loo, she thought wildly, and come back and tell him her period had started, goodbye and it's been nice knowing you!

She tightened her mouth to stop it wobbling in plain panic and wild indecision and Sebastian told her flatly, 'We'll stay at my mother's home just outside Jerez. You'll have company—Marcus is there with his fiancée-to-be. He's easy to get on with and, ostensibly, you'll be there to help Terrina get organised for the move back to England.' He laid down his fork, his plate empty. 'Packing and so forth, running errands. She'll like the idea of having a personal maid,' he informed her drily. 'I have business to attend to back home, so my early return won't cause undue comment.'

He sighed. He hadn't meant to, but the thought of the devious methods he would have to employ to get rid of Terrina stuck in his gullet like a spectacularly sour plum.

A sizzle of something that was part excitement, part trepidation, fizzed through every last one of Rosie's veins. It was scary, but she could do it. She could.

She could put up with being an unwanted nuisance as far as Sebastian was concerned for the chance to come face to face with her father at last.

She picked up her fork and said, tonelessly, she hoped, 'OK, I'll tag along. When do we leave?'

CHAPTER SIX

WHEN Sebastian slid the sleekly opulent car into a reserved spot in the underground car park and, carrying her tatty luggage, ushered her into the matt steel lift that whisked them up into an ultra-modern, fabulously expensive penthouse suite Rosie's embarrassment deepened until it practically sucked her into its hot and squirmy depths.

Acres of bare polished wood flooring, a group of small sofas upholstered in an ultra-soft black leather which sported the slightest and most tasteful sheen, low clean-lined tables, artful spot lighting, two modern paintings which she guessed would just have to be masterpieces and worth a small fortune, even though she couldn't make head nor tail of them.

The apartment he used when he was in London, Sebastian had informed her. He also had a house in Cadiz. Well, bully for him!

It was all a far cry from the run-down estate where she had been brought up. She'd seen his eyes narrow as he'd taken in the sight of the groups of mean-looking youths lounging on street corners, the younger kids kicking empty beer cans about, the abandoned cars on the waste land that had once been a kiddies' playground but was now, somehow, turned into a rubbish dump.

'I'll show you where you'll be sleeping.' His voice sounded flat. As if, Rosie thought miserably, he was now regretting having ever suggested she accompany him to Spain, where she would sully the rarefied atmosphere of his mother's no doubt exquisite home.

Rosie followed like an automaton. She'd had to call in to collect her passport and pack a few more things for the journey ahead, there had been no getting out of it. Not that she was ashamed of her home ground but it made the differences between them stand out even more starkly.

Man-like, he'd told her to get her passport, not to bother with anything else, no doubt blithely thinking she could manage with just the working jeans and tops she'd taken to Troone Manor.

And man-like again, stubbornly refusing to stay with the car as she'd suggested, in case someone stole the wheels, he had followed her into the mini-market, chatting with Jeff, who was manning the check-out, while she shot up to her room, Jean hot on her tail.

'Do you know what you're doing?' her old friend had demanded. 'He could be a white slaver, for all I know! Now your mother's gone, God rest her, I feel responsible for you.'

'He's my employer.' Rosie had pushed her passport into her best handbag, added a couple of clean handkerchiefs and her purse, which felt comfortably fat with her week's earnings, solemnly counted out by Madge. 'Going to Spain is the only way I'll ever clap eyes on Marcus Troone. He's not in England.' She'd reached down a shabby suitcase from the top of the wardrobe and stuffed everything she owned into it, just in case, patiently explaining, 'Apparently, he was taken ill a while back and is getting his strength back over there. It was either grab the opportunity or forget all about getting to meet him. You don't have to worry about me, truly you don't.'

'Well, if you're sure.' Jean hadn't sounded very convinced. 'Keep in touch, won't you? You have our phone number. And Rosie—don't think I forgot your birthday. I didn't. I didn't send a card or phone you. I didn't know if you'd gone there incognito and I didn't want to blow your cover! But I'd planned a surprise party for when you got back here.'

Touched, Rosie had flung her arms around her old friend's neck, miserably aware of how disappointed in her she'd be if she knew how closely she'd followed in her mother's footsteps and jumped into bed with a man who was so completely out of her league.

Uncomfortably aware now that the proximity of a bed and Sebastian Garcia was having a terrible effect on her heart-rate, she shuffled her feet against the thick pile of the white carpet. As if sensing her discomfiture he turned the brilliance of his silver eyes on her and she shivered, knowing that her determination to get real and wipe all her immature yearnings out of her head was a lost cause. Hell would freeze over before she would stop wanting him for herself, loving him.

'It's too late to do anything useful today. I'll phone out for our supper and we'll go shopping tomorrow.' His dark drawl made her spine quiver and her fascinated gaze lingered helplessly on the taut powerful lines of his body as he placed her luggage at the foot of the bed, where the battered old suitcase and the bulging plastic carrier reminded her shamefully of a heap of clutter left out for the bin men.

Knowing that something other than an embarrassed

silence would naturally be expected of her, Rosie hauled herself together and countered, 'How long are we going to be here?' Then, remembering what he'd said about going to the shops, she offered, 'If you'll tell me how to get to a supermarket I'll do the shopping if you like. I'm a dab hand at finding bargains, believe me.' That way she wouldn't feel quite such a hanger-on. She could make herself useful and save him money by cooking for them instead of him having to send out for stuff that would probably be horribly expensive.

Sebastian tossed her an underbrow look as a huge wave of tenderness engulfed him. She was obviously feeling out of her depth, anxious to slip into a role she would be comfortable with. A skivvy. Well, no way. She deserved better. She deserved the best.

And quite where that thought had come from, or why it was so insistent, he had no idea. But he gave her his heartbreaking smile, and said, 'We're not going shopping for food, *cara*. I want to see you wearing decent clothes. You have a beautiful body; it's a crime to hide it under dull, practical working gear. And we'll only be in London until I can arrange our flight out.' He shot a look at his slim gold wristwatch. 'Which I'm about to get on to now.'

Poleaxed by what had sounded like an endearment and a very real compliment, Rosie went bright scarlet and was too tongue-tied to speak until he'd turned on his heel and made a swift exit.

By the time she'd gathered herself she could already hear him speaking on the phone, so that put paid to her belated intention to run after him and explain that she couldn't afford to buy new clothes.

Besides, she surely had something she could wear without making him cringe with embarrassment at being seen out with her.

Staunchly determined not to read too much into what he'd said about her having a beautiful body, because men who leapt into bed with women on practically their first meeting probably said that sort of thing all the time, she began the dispiriting task of unpacking.

Rosie had been awake for what seemed like absolutely ages but she wasn't nearly ready to leave her bed and face the rest of the day. With him.

Yesterday evening had been bad enough; the hours and hours stretching ahead would be worse.

After he'd shown her to the room she was to use, she'd left him to his phoning and whatever else he was doing, too uncomfortable with the situation to be easy in his company. To pass the time, and hopefully stop herself thinking about him, she'd had a shower in the adjoining *en suite* bathroom, pampering herself with the fragrant shampoos, oils and essences that would normally be way beyond her means.

And, just to show him she had something other than shabby old jeans and sweatshirts to wear, she'd got into her one good dress. Bought several years ago because she'd fallen in love with the colour, a lovely hyacinth-blue, and she'd needed one nice dress to take on the school trip to Paris, it had been a real bargain. Not second-hand, either, but a knock-down price in a closing down sale.

She had cinched the belt as tight as it would go. She'd obviously lost quite a bit of weight since she'd worn it last. But teamed with her respectable brown shoes she did look presentable. Not sophisticated or expensive, of course, as the women Sebastian would be used to squiring around would be expected to look, but nothing to be ashamed of, either.

She'd been a bundle of nerves when he'd finally rapped on her bedroom door and told her, a touch impatiently, that their supper had arrived. Half hoping that he'd approve of the way she looked, and announce that in his opinion she didn't need to spend her precious wages on clothes she obviously didn't need, she had been disproportionately disappointed when he had said nothing at all.

Seated opposite him at the kitchen table—the room resembled a set for an avant garde space-age film, she decided—her appetite had fled. She had been sure the food was delicious, the Sebastian Garcias of this world wouldn't ruin their superior palates with anything suspect from a greasy spoon takeaway, but apart from nibbling at a giant prawn in a lemony sauce she hadn't been able to eat a thing.

'We fly out the day after tomorrow,' was the only thing he said to her, not sounding over the moon about it, either, and for the rest of the time he seemed preoccupied with troublesome thoughts that he obviously had no intention of sharing with her. Growing more hot under the collar by the second, Rosie decided she knew why.

Sitting up very straight, she told him, 'Look, if you're having second thoughts about my going with you to Spain, just say so. I'm not exactly thrilled about it, either.'

Pushing his own barely touched plate away,

Sebastian released a long sigh, his lean face hardening, his eyes pinning her to her seat. 'Backing out, Rosie?'

His tone warned her that if she gave him an affirmative she'd be in for a rough ride. And if she did back out she would lose the opportunity of seeing her father. Her own flesh and blood.

But that didn't really matter, did it? She could always visit Troone Manor when Marcus was back in residence and decide whether or not to introduce herself according to what her instincts at the time told her.

She didn't know why she hadn't thought of that simple option before, and having an option gave her the courage to point out kindly, 'I expect you find me a nuisance. I know why you feel you have to keep an eye on me—we both behaved stupidly—' oh, lordy, why did she have to keep blushing? She must resemble a boiled lobster! 'But if I give you my solemn word that I'll write and put you in the picture, when I know what the picture is, you needn't go to the trouble of hauling me all the way to Spain.'

Her breath gone, she sagged feebly back in her seat, what she had just done hitting her right in the face. She'd given him the perfect get-out and she knew she didn't want him to take it. She was every kind of fool! Didn't she know that spending time around him was damaging her poor demented heart? Of course she damned well did!

So, it had to be said, if he took up her offer to write with any news she had and put her on the first train back to Wolverhampton in the morning, she might not like it, and would probably cry her eyes out for a month, but he would be doing her a kindness.

He just kept looking at her, as if, she thought dejectedly, he was wondering if he could trust her to keep her word. She wriggled in her seat. Her emotions were going all chaotic again, as they normally did around this man, and when he tonelessly remarked, ''Hauling' you to Spain, as you so elegantly put it, will be no trouble at all,' there was nothing else for it but to push back her chair, bid him a stiff goodnight, and head with more speed than dignity to her room. At least his attitude told her he had no intention of making love to her again. He didn't repeat his mistakes. The knowledge should have made her feel more comfortable about the situation. But it didn't.

Now it was almost ten in the morning. She wasn't used to staying in bed late, but the thought of enduring hours and hours of Sebastian's stone-faced silences kept her where she was.

It was perfectly obvious that he didn't trust her to keep her word. He didn't know her so why should he trust her? She didn't know him, either, so she didn't know what he'd meant when he'd said he took his responsibilities seriously.

How could two people who didn't know the first thing about each other fall into bed, just like that?

She squirmed under the duvet, freshly awash with shame, and made the humiliating mental note that he hadn't contradicted her when she'd said that he must find her a nuisance.

An omission brought home to her when, after what she quiveringly decided was a most perfunctory rap, he strode into the room and drawled, 'Shake a leg, Nuisance! I'm taking you to breakfast.'

Between the strands of rumpled blonde hair that fell over her forehead and the top of the duvet she had pulled right up to her nose and was hanging on to for grim life, her sapphire eyes widened at him and she felt her whole body relax for the first time since she'd woken hours ago. His devastating smile and the fascinatingly warm glints in his black fringed silvery eyes told her he was teasing about the nuisance bit.

She couldn't begin to understand him. Last night he'd barely been able to bring himself to speak to her and now he was all smiles, teasing her. It was his volatile Spanish temperament, she guessed. Whatever, she wasn't going to knock it!

Her eyes were sparkling at him, come-to-bed eyes. Sebastian's throat went tight. Her lovely hair was all over the place. His fingers ached to touch it, smooth it away from her face, to peel the duvet away from her slender but perfect body, to lose himself in her again.

Bunching his treacherous hands in the side pockets of his suit trousers, Sebastian turned abruptly away from a temptation he was having difficulty resisting, and said flatly, 'Wear something warm; it's cold out.' He closed the door with deliberate quietness behind him and strode, tight-lipped, to the kitchen and the pot of hot coffee he'd made before waking her.

Ten minutes later Rosie tracked him down. Sprawled out at the kitchen table, he was staring moodily into a mug of black coffee. He hadn't heard her enter and for a few moments she allowed herself the luxury of just looking at him.

He was so attractive he made her head spin and her heart jump right up into her throat. Wearing a mid-grey suit, immaculately tailored to his lithe body, a paler grey shirt and deep blue silk tie, he literally took her breath away.

The only thing that marred the effect of suave masculine perfection was the tousled state of his raven hair. Had he been running frantic fingers through it, reducing its normally expensively barbered state to something that resembled a wind tossed haystack? It gave him an endearing look of vulnerability that turned her insides over.

How could such a gorgeous guy have found her desirable enough to make love to her? If she hadn't known it had happened she would have said it was impossible. Unless, and the thought drained her, he had simply wanted sex and any available woman would have done.

She must have made some sound because he turned and looked at her, his wide hard mouth flat and tight. She saw his eyes raking her, taking in her most presentable jeans, the anorak worn over the scarlet woolly jumper Jean had knitted for her last Christmas. Whether it was the contrast between her plain ordinariness and his own Savile Row urbanity, she had no way of knowing. Whatever, she could read his moody, narrowed eyes well enough to know that there was some kind of battle going on inside that handsome head.

She hadn't realised she'd been holding her breath beneath his raking scrutiny until she saw his tense shoulders relax, his mouth soften into a half-smile as he got fluidly to his feet.

Sebastian covered the distance between them in three smooth strides. Selfishly, he'd been too twisted up in his own convoluted and confused thought processes for the past twenty-four hours to give any thought to what she must be feeling, had spent far too much time trying to sort his head out.

She was alone in the world, probably scared silly at the prospect of possible pregnancy, out of her depth and nervous about spending the next couple of weeks in a foreign country with people who were strangers to her.

He had to reassure her, put her at her ease. Make her understand that he would take care of her. A warm glow centred in the region of his heart. Caring for her wouldn't present a problem—so long as he could handle his libido, he amended wryly.

Reaching a soft white handkerchief from his pocket, he shook out the folds and gently rubbed her mouth, removing all traces of the bright orange lipstick she had plastered all over it, carefully avoiding the stunned shock in her beautiful eyes.

At least she wasn't wearing that awful cheap dress. It had been several sizes too big, badly made, and the purply blue colour hadn't done a thing for her. When she'd walked in wearing it another of those giant waves of tenderness had swamped him. He'd wanted to rip the offensive thing off her back and dress her in the best that money could buy, pay tribute to her loveliness.

Well, the thought was father to the deed, wasn't it? Producing a flat tone, he informed her, 'That's better.' He dropped his hands and made a show of consulting his watch again. 'The limo should be waiting now.

Hungry?' A casual hand on the small of her back urged her to the vestibule and the waiting lift, and Rosie went, feeling all tangled up inside.

Her soft lips felt swollen, sensitised. As if he had kissed her. What he'd done had felt so—so intimate and really erotic she admitted to herself on a quiver of hopelessly futile excitement.

When all it had really meant was that he didn't like to see women wearing make-up. She had thought the splash of vivid colour had made her look less as if she was part of the woodwork.

When he ushered her into the rear of the waiting chauffeur-driven limo she gathered up her wandering wits and wanted to know, 'Why hire this package when you've a very nice car of your own?'

Sliding back the glass partition, Sebastian gave the driver a series of instructions, then settled back beside her as the big car purred away to join the traffic. 'Because I dislike driving in London. It takes too much concentration and today I want to concentrate on you.'

That piece of information flustered her. Almost as much as the close proximity of his lean and powerful frame, the long legs stretched out in front of him, the expensive fabric clinging lovingly to his thighs. Naked, those thighs were hot and hard, roughened with dark body hair. A far too vivid memory of how they had felt entwined with her own made her go hot all over.

She swallowed convulsively, felt her face flame, and looked quickly away. Almost before she knew it the car was stationary, Sebastian sliding out and opening the door at her side.

They were in a side street, and even she knew you weren't allowed to park on double yellow lines. They were standing outside a café with steamed up windows and handwritten notices in alarming colours giving the prices of this and that.

Bemused, Rosie glanced up at him and felt a smile creep over her face. Provided she could stop herself having wicked thoughts about him, the day ahead might not be the ordeal she'd lain in bed dreading.

He looked really relaxed and much more approachable than he had done yesterday, and as the car eased back into the traffic he smiled down at her. 'The driver will be back to collect us in three quarters of an hour.' He draped a companionable arm around her shoulders. 'Let's eat, shall we? It might look like a dump, but I can assure you the food might be basic but it's very good.'

It might look like a dump to Sebastian Garcia, but it suited Rosie just fine: the steamy atmosphere, the smell of bacon and coffee, the plastic chairs set around formica-topped tables, the big jovial man in the crumpled white overall who seemed to be in charge. He greeted Sebastian like a long-lost brother and Rosie, settling herself at a vacant table by the window, her stomach rumbling with sudden hunger, felt swept away by happiness.

This super wealthy, knock-'em-dead-handsome Spaniard hadn't brought her here because he was ashamed to be seen with her anywhere more exclusive. He wasn't a snob. He was well known by the owner so he must eat here often when he was in London. She felt warm and glowing all over. Nicely relaxed for a change.

And the full English breakfast when it arrived was perfectly cooked and so lavish that she couldn't manage the toast and marmalade that came after it, although Sebastian did it justice. Comfortably replete, she reached her purse from her handbag. 'We'll go Dutch, shall we?' she offered brightly.

'Please don't insult me, *cara*.' The delivery was low voiced but so harsh that not even the endearment could soften it. The happiness of the interlude was wiped away. The way they'd talked of this and that so easily, his descriptions of his home in Cadiz, the ancient fountain in the inner courtyard, the fact that you could actually walk outside any time you liked and pick an orange from your own tree sounded wonderful. He'd promised to take her there. She couldn't wait.

Now the easy closeness had been swept away by a few tightly voiced words, making her feel gauche and faintly ridiculous. He screwed up his paper napkin and said, 'The driver will be here in a few moments.'

Her voice emerged stiffly as she countered, 'Why? Where are we supposed to be going?'

'Shopping. For clothes. I told you.' Fishing a twenty-pound note out of an inner pocket, he laid it on the table and anchored it beneath the plastic sauce dispenser that was shaped like a huge tomato.

Rosie, her small face flaming, muttered crossly, 'I don't need any. I can't afford to buy stuff I don't need.'

'Probably not,' he conceded. 'But I can. Humour me.'

'No.' Rosie was adamant. She wasn't going to let him buy clothes for her. It didn't feel right. Unless—

Her pulse-rate rocketing, she pushed out, genuinely appalled, 'What are you trying to do? Pay me off?' She'd read about men like that. They had affairs which ended with a gift. A big fat jewel or a flash new car. Only she'd been a one-night stand so a new dress should suffice!

'Don't,' He ran the tip of his forefinger along her flaming cheekbone. 'It's true, I feel guilty as hell about what I did,' he told her quietly. 'Nothing can make me feel better about that. But, I promise you, my only motive is to see your beautiful body in clothes that do it justice. So I ask you again, humour me in this?'

She couldn't doubt his sincerity. It reverberated in his smoky voice and shone from his eyes. Melting because he thought her beautiful, she drew her lower lip between her teeth and, against all her principles, found herself weakly capitulating as she probably always would do with this man because, loving the wretch, she couldn't help wanting to please him. Her eyes downcast, shadowed with the knowledge that she was a hopeless case, she nodded mutely.

'*Bueno,*' he murmured, then his irresistible grin flashed as he held out a hand to help her to her feet, disarming her utterly. It was a knack he had, she thought defeatedly. 'Promise me one thing more, Rosie—relax and enjoy the experience?'

Amazingly, she did. Once she had got over her initial uneasiness at being ushered into a glass and marble salon, with a bunch of superior-looking beings hovering over her, picking up strands of her hair, turning her head this way and that and peering at her skin, she just let go, took an interest and enjoyed the novel experience of being the pampered centre of interest.

And the girl who had shown her how to use make-up had been really nice and, in between their animated conversation about her pair of Siamese cats and Rosie's confession that when she had a place of her own she would definitely go for one of that breed, plus a dog, or maybe two, she had explained which colours suited Rosie and which would not. Bright orange or scarlet lipsticks being ruled right out of play.

Her eyes still sparkling, her pink-glossed lips curved in a smile of pure pleasure, her hair, which had been layered so that it swung smoothly around her face, feeling cleaner and shinier than it had ever felt before, she joined Sebastian in the reception area.

Laying aside the broadsheet he'd been reading, he rose to his feet, unaware, apparently, of the interest of every female in the area, and gave her a nod of approval.

Tucking her hand beneath his arm, he escorted her to the door and Rosie felt dizzy with pride. She was the envy of the women who were waiting for their appointments. No one had ever envied her before! She was walking on air.

And hadn't managed to float back to earth when she was whisked away to a shop that didn't look like any shop she'd ever seen before—wall to wall soft dove-grey carpet, tall mirrors in ornate gilt frames, comfy two-seater sofas upholstered in cream-coloured fabric, an enormous crystal chandelier hanging from the high ceiling.

At a gesture from him she sank down on one of the sofas while he went to talk to the regal-looking woman dressed in stark black who had glided forward. It appeared to be a serious discussion; Rosie wondered what on earth they were finding to talk about, and came back down to earth with a bang when the regal lady looked in her direction and actually sneered! At least, that was what it looked like from where she was sitting.

Sneered at her old brown anorak? The poor woman had probably never before seen such a downmarket object in her hallowed space! She swallowed a hysterical giggle and her mouth was still wobbling when Sebastian finally joined her. To stop herself from bursting into a humiliating mixture of wild laughter and fountains of tears that would get them both thrown out on to the street, she watched the regal lady disappear through a gap between the mirrors and grumped at him, 'I don't know what you think we're doing here. Let's get out. Quick. Before she comes back. I don't need or want a new dress, or whatever. And I feel such a fool!'

His long mouth twitching, silver eyes dancing, he captured her chin between his forefinger and thumb. '*Silencio*. And stop putting yourself down. You're far from being a fool, so how could you look like one? Besides, I don't want the maybe-mother of my child looking like a tramp.'

Rosie swallowed. Hard. She struggled to absorb what had sounded like a very backhanded compliment. Difficult when she was totally absorbed in the electrifying sensations engendered by the touch of his lean fingers against her skin.

'Don't!' she muttered, twisting her head away from that totally enervating touch, knotting her fingers in her lap. 'Don't talk like that! There probably won't be a baby. And what happened was as much my fault as yours. You didn't force yourself on me, remember? Anyway, how would you like it if I took you some place and made you sit like a lemon while I bought you some new trousers, or vests, or something?'

Right on cue the regal lady returned, just as Sebastian flung back his dark head and roared with laughter. And it was just as well, otherwise she would most definitely have slapped his handsome face!

As it was, she had to contain herself. She couldn't slap him in front of an audience. And there were two of them now, a perfectly manicured thirty-something in a very elegant black suit pulling a fancy-looking dress rail behind her, crammed with garments on padded hangers.

One by one the hangers were removed, the garments reverently held out for Sebastian's inspection by the older woman. Those he nodded at were put back on the rail. A shake of the head had the thirty-something stepping forward to receive the unapproved whatever and drape it over her arm.

Not that there were too many of those, Rosie decided, wondering what he was playing at. Everything she had seen was mouthwatering, but useless. When would she ever get to wear something that reeked of good taste and a bottomless pocket?

When she found herself in a fitting room as large as a normal person's sitting room, surrounded by mirrors, accompanied by the fancy dress rail, she gritted her teeth and got on with it.

She was supposed to try everything on and parade in front of him—presumably so he could make his choice—she, obviously, had no say in the matter, she thought mutinously, determined to be as quick as she could about it. Humouring Sebastian Garcia certainly had a big downside.

Telling the surprised thirty-something that she didn't need any help, but it was nice of her to offer, Rosie stripped down to her serviceable white cotton bra and briefs and pulled on the first thing that came to hand, carefully not looking at herself in the mirrors.

She didn't want to see herself wearing fabulous clothes. She might get to covet them. She was happy with her lifestyle as it was. She didn't want to want things she could never have.

Like Sebastian. The thought made her feel ill. She pushed it firmly out of her head and went on with the silly charade of parading the whole selection in front of him.

No comment. Just the slow drift of his eyes over whatever she happened to be wearing at the time. Someone had given him a flute of champagne. All right for some! He was having a nice relaxing cold drink while she was going demented!

Stripping, she dived into the last thing on the rail. A beautiful suit in soft cream cashmere. She buttoned the jacket, trying hard not to love the way it felt as if it had been made just for her. There was a selection of shoes in all styles and colours, presumably to go with all the different outfits. She hadn't worn any of them. She wasn't wearing stockings, so she couldn't, so she'd padded out in her navy blue socks, not looking at the regal lady, because she just knew she'd be sneering.

'Keep that on.' It was the first remark he'd made.

Rosie nearly fainted with relief. While she hadn't wanted him to buy a single thing for her, she'd been feeling more and more agitated at his seeming total lack of enthusiasm for any of the things she'd modelled. The queenly owner of the establishment would have been seriously miffed if she'd gone to all this trouble and Sebastian had turned down everything she'd had to offer.

Back in the changing room she looked at her reflection and was definitely shocked. The suit was really gorgeous. It made her look classy. She could scarcely believe she was seeing herself.

A pair of taupe leather classic courts with two-inch heels was produced, together with a pair of sheer tights, and Rosie accepted them from the now smiling regal lady with relief. She hoped Sebastian wouldn't grumble at the extra expense but it would have been sacrilege to wear her clumpy brown lace-ups and navy socks with such a beautiful work of art.

A grin split Sebastian's face as Rosie rejoined him. He'd been spot-on. Wearing the right clothes and make-up, she looked absolutely stunning. A truly classy beauty with a sparkle, an inner warmth that other perfectly packaged and groomed females of his acquaintance signally lacked.

He narrowed his eyes and ate her up. The soft colour on her delicate cheekbones owed nothing to artificial blusher and her glossy, full lips were slightly parted, hovering on a smile. He could see the intriguing pulse-beat at the base of her elegant throat where the suit jacket parted in a discreet V, just hinting at the naked delights beneath the soft fabric.

His blood heated, charged through his veins, and if

he didn't switch his mind to something else, pronto, he was going to embarrass himself. Hugely.

Avoiding her radiant eyes, he stared at that pulse-beat. There was something lacking. Something else he could do. Something that would take his mind off sex.

Roughly clearing his throat, he gave her his arm to hang on to. 'Let's go!' He swept her out to the waiting limo. 'We need to be some place else.'

CHAPTER SEVEN

MADRE DI DIO! It hadn't worked.

Neither had the long walk they'd taken in Regents Park after the visit to the jeweller's.

Sebastian ended the call he'd been making to the firm of caterers he always used when he entertained at his London apartment, thrust his slim mobile into his inner breast pocket and joined Rosie in the back of the limo. At least the caterer's presence this evening would ensure he didn't jump her.

He frowned. He hoped it would.

He'd intended to take her out for dinner, somewhere glitzy, to see and be seen, but the way his body kept reacting had ruled that right out of play. The idea of making a fool of himself in a public place—which, given the state of his libido, he probably would—gave him the shudders.

Leaning forward, he gave the driver his instructions and had a vivid mental flashback of Rosie running to the front of the car and telling the stuffily correct chauffeur when he'd dropped them off for that walk in the park, 'We've not stopped for lunch because we had a huge breakfast. But I'm sure you must be starving. We won't mind waiting while you go and get something to eat.'

She'd looked so concerned, her lovely head tipped to one side, and not altogether convinced when the starchy, impeccably uniformed man had immediately thawed, his craggy face transformed by a fatherly grin as he'd confided, 'That's thoughtful of you, madam. But the missus always makes me a packed lunch. You just enjoy your walk now.'

Sebastian slid the glass panel back into place and subsided against the leather upholstery. When had he ever heard his date concern herself about the well-being of another human being, let alone someone she would consider to be a humble minion and so far beneath her they weren't worth noticing?

Never. Ever.

Aware of every breath she took, he glared straight ahead, not trusting himself to look at her.

He wanted to have sex with her. Here. Now.

Oblivious, Rosie fingered the fine gold chain around her neck. Sebastian had insisted on buying it; he'd whisked her into a jeweller's and had taken ages making his selection. Then, when he'd lifted her hair and fastened the cool gold links around her neck, the heated brush of his fingers on her nape had made her breasts strain against her suit jacket which, as it had happened, had been pressed against his chest. She hoped he hadn't noticed.

She hadn't wanted him to spend any more money on her, and she'd told him so, but she'd had to agree with him that the chain did set the suit off beautifully.

The lovely suit would wear out eventually, but the gold chain would last for ever. If she ever had a daughter she would pass it on to her, she decided dreamily. And tell her how it had been given to her by the most handsome man ever to walk the planet, a man she had only known briefly but had loved with all of her heart.

Shades of her own mother! Her hand dropped heavily to her lap. Maybe she was already carrying that daughter. Sebastian's child.

Oh, my goodness! Her face flooded with heat. It wasn't remotely sensible, but she passionately hoped so! Any child of his would be utterly adorable, a part of him that would be hers for always.

A sudden flash of inspiration made the breath snag in her throat. Turning to him, she gazed at his hard, set profile, her voice low even though she knew the driver, behind his glass partition, couldn't hear her, 'We've been really dim! You can buy something to test for pregnancy at any chemist, can't you? Then we'd know for sure, wouldn't we?'

Yeah. Right.

Sebastian felt her eyes on him and didn't move. Stared ahead at the back of the driver's neck.

And the morning after pill. Don't forget that. It had been the first thing he'd thought about. And immediately discounted.

Because subconsciously he'd wanted her to be carrying his child?

And he'd ruled out a pregnancy test. Because he'd needed an excuse to keep her with him?

Doing a test had only just occurred to her. Her naivety was one of the thousands of things he liked about her. With a smothered groan he turned to her. He ached to take her in his arms. She gave him an encouraging smile. Sebastian shuddered; she had no idea what she was doing to him. She was probably expecting him to instruct the driver to stop at the first chemist's shop they came to. And he knew then that whether she was pregnant or not he wanted to keep her with him.

And it wasn't just sex. There was a lot more to it than that.

He closed his eyes, his jaw tightening. The need to take her in his arms, hold her, kiss her senseless, was fiercely strong, and it was probably just as well they were now sweeping into the underground parking lot of the apartment block. He was going to have to think long and hard about what he really wanted, no jumping in feet first. He'd done that ten years ago, landed a cropper and learned a useful lesson.

But Rosie wasn't like Magdalena, or any of the other glossy harpies who had cash registers for hearts—

'Sir?'

Aware that he was still glaring straight ahead, that Rosie had exited the car and the driver was holding the door for him, Sebastian got a firm hold on himself. He'd already been more than rash where Rosie was concerned. The little fact that his behaviour had been unprecedented was neither here nor there. He had to use his head, not think with his hormones.

Concluding his business with the driver, he escorted Rosie to the lift. His subconscious might have dismissed the pregnancy test but it was time his clear-thinking logical mind took control. There would be time to purchase the necessary first thing in the morning and do the test before their flight left at midday.

Ignoring the sour lurch of his guts produced by the fact that if the test turned up negative her ticket on the flight to Jerez wouldn't be used because as far as she was concerned she would have no need to accompany him, he allowed her to precede him into the small foyer of his apartment.

His head told him that in that event she would have no cause for complaint. His former lovers would have been satisfied with what he had done for little Rosie Lambert today. He knew, down to the last cent, the price demanded at the end of the affair, and what had happened with Rosie could hardly be called that.

So why did his heart sing to a different tune?

'Oh, my giddy aunt!' In front of him Rosie stumbled awkwardly and Sebastian instinctively steadied her, clamping both hands around her tiny waist to stop her from falling. 'Who left all this stuff here?'

She knew she sounded as if all the breath had whooshed out of her lungs and hoped he'd put it down to her having nearly fallen flat on her face over the mounds of boxes and distinctively elegant carriers filling the floor space, and not guess that the dominating pressure of his long supple hands around her waist was responsible for some sort of cataclysmic internal explosion.

'Whatever is it?' she squawked, and hated herself for her total lack of cool.

'Do you really have to ask?' he parried curtly, immediately dropping his hands. The warmth of her body was stealing through her jacket, scorching his skin. Stuffing his hands in his trouser pockets, out of harm's way, he stepped over the pile. 'I had them delivered. The janitor has a key. I suggest you sort through them and pack what you'll need for Spain.'

He clamped his mouth on the words, but he couldn't take them back. She might not be accompanying him to his mother's home, might she?

Cursing himself for allowing her to tie him in knots, he offered tersely, 'I'll help you carry them to your room,' and met her wide, shocked eyes.

'You can't!'

All those clothes? All the things he'd given the nod to? Everything she'd modelled for him?

She was horrified. The stuff must have cost a bomb! Accepting the suit and the gold chain had made her uncomfortable. Accepting this lot was completely out of the question.

Ignoring the anguished look in her beautiful sapphire eyes, he deliberately misread her blurted statement, bending to lift a stack of boxes. 'I'm not in my dotage. I'm capable of carrying a few boxes,' he told her curtly, turned his back on her and strode towards her bedroom.

'But—' Dismayed, she scurried after him. He'd put the distinctive gold and white boxes on the bed and was already removing the tops. 'I didn't mean you were too feeble to carry them,' she snapped. 'You know I didn't!' She planted her feet apart and folded her arms high across her chest. 'I can't accept this stuff. It's way too much. And I'd never get to wear it, in any case. It's such a waste. Send it all back!'

'Can't. And it's no use to me.' Sebastian straightened, the gold tissue evening dress that had made her look so stunningly spectacular dangling from his fingers, taking in her confrontational stance. Warmth flooded his heart, spread rapidly through his veins, prompting him to murmur huskily, 'I'm not into cross-dressing.' He badly wanted to see her answering radiant smile.

For a moment Rosie was severely tempted into succumbing to the laughter lights in those compelling silver eyes, to the twitch of humour that softened the hard sensual lines of his kissable mouth. She resisted with difficulty. This was a serious issue.

Injecting scorn into her voice, she ignored his crack about cross-dressing and reminded him, 'You invented my cover story, remember? I'm suppose to be some sort of ladies' maid.'

Her upper lip curled with unhidden distaste. The more she thought about the role she would be expected to play, the less she liked it. But it would give her the chance to see her father and, hopefully, get an inkling of what he was like.

Her duplicity in this had her not liking herself very much and had her tacking on in defensive grumpiness, 'I should look humble, so instead of all this—' a wild sweep of one arm indicated the results of his morning's misguided shopping spree 'you should have bought a plain black dress and a neat white pinny and maybe thrown in a sensible nylon overall for when I'm cleaning the lady's shoes!'

Her reminder came like a slap on the face. The thought of this beautiful creature in a menial capacity, at the beck and call of a woman like Terrina, left a poisonous taste in his mouth.

His lips flattened savagely. 'Change of plan. I don't know why I came up with that scenario. You will be going to my country with me as my guest. A true equal in every way there is.' His eyes glittered. 'And, on the subject of cleaning her shoes, Terrina's not fit to so much as touch yours.'

'Wow!' Rosie expelled a long, pent-up breath, her eyes widening. He looked all simmering, potent male.

And did he really regard her as his equal? The very idea made her tremble. She had fallen in love with a man so far above her class that the idea of him introducing her as his guest was difficult to assimilate.

She saw the tension leave his wide shoulders, saw his rock-hard features relax into a sudden smile. And when he held out the dress he'd been holding and said, 'Wear this for me tonight. We're eating in. The caterers will be arriving soon. I'll bring the rest of the stuff through,' her whole body was flooded with such a strange excitement she felt she was floating, out of control, a puppet being pulled by a master's strings.

An hour later she surveyed her reflection and tried to control the persistent wriggle of excitement that was squirming around in her stomach.

She hardly recognised herself. She looked expensive, special. Her hair shimmered, a soft pale gold, and the chain glittered against her throat. And the dress was out-of-this-world, the gold tissue halter straps fastening neatly at her nape softly widening, clinging to the curve of her breasts to meet the narrow waistline and fall sleekly to the knee-length hemline of the skirt.

Her back was bare to just above her waist, so she hadn't been able to wear one of the lacy bras she'd found in one of the carriers. Just a filmy pair of briefs, a wicked suspender belt and a pair of sheer silk stockings.

She felt like a kept woman. A pampered, indulged mistress. She caught the reflected and definitely sinful curve of her full pink lips, quelled any lingering misgivings and decided that, for tonight at least, she wasn't going to knock it. She would go with this wildly excited, scary feeling; she would pretend she really was special, the Spaniard's woman.

Tomorrow would be soon enough to plonk her feet firmly back on the ground, to nip out and buy that pregnancy test thing, and if it was negative put plan B into action—visiting Troone Manor when she knew her father was back there.

And if it was positive? Well, just for tonight she wasn't going to think about that.

'Señor Garcia is in the living area, madam.'

'Oh. Right. Thanks.' Flicking the white-coated waiter an apologetic smile, Rosie backed out of the kitchen. She wasn't wanted there. The space-age film set had been taken over by the caterers. A smart young waiter had been pulling on his white gloves and an efficient-looking woman was doing something with a stainless steel dish and the state-of-the-art oven.

Swaying on the three-inch heels of her gold kid shoes, she headed for the living room, the softly shimmering fabric of her skirt brushing sensuously against her silk-clad legs. It made her feel turned on. As if to prove that unfortunate state of affairs her breasts tingled, hardened and peaked against the gossamer-fine barrier of her halter top, and she shivered even as a light beading of perspiration adorned her short upper lip.

Heaven help her! This dress was wicked! She should have pushed it back into its folds of tissue paper, stuffed it back in its box and clambered into her old jeans and jumper. He had commanded and she'd jumped, more fool her. Because just look where besotted obedience had got her—all dolled up like a dog's dinner, fantasising about being the Spaniard's woman!

As if!

In increasing turmoil, Rosie pushed open the door, and the sight of an immaculately dinner-suited Sebastian staring out of one of the tall windows at the million city lights spread out beneath him didn't settle her nerves one tiny little bit.

He had his back to her. The commanding width of his shoulders, the way his body tapered to narrow hips and the length of his elegantly trousered legs made her mouth run dry. He was such a beautiful specimen of dominant masculinity he made her head spin and her poor heart beat like a steam hammer.

And then he turned, even though she'd been really quiet, hovering in the doorway like a paralysed mouse, and she glimpsed the hard, set features of his angular face for a split second before his hooded silver eyes made a comprehensive sweep of her now drastically overheated body. And then he smiled. A slow, sultry curving of that sensual mouth. It blew her mind.

'You are gorgeous, *cara mia*.' He held out his hand. 'Come to me.'

His low sexy drawl should have unsettled her even further but it did no such thing. It washed through her veins like wildfire and made her heart sing. Plunged back into fantasy land, she obeyed his command and walked towards him, but slowly, submitting to his will but sensing a glorious power of her own for the very first time in her life.

A power in the way he watched her every movement, the lowering of his eyelids so that the slits of silver were intensified to a fevered brilliance beneath the thick dark sweep of his lashes. A power in the way the faint dull flush of male desire across his angular slashing cheekbones betrayed him.

The whisper of the costly fabric against her silk-covered legs, the way he was looking at her—as if he were drawn into her magical fantasy—made her shatteringly aware of her femininity. And when his outstretched hand reached for hers she stopped breathing. The electrically charged touch of warm skin and hard bone told her she was playing with fire.

And it was addictive.

'Never let anyone tell you you are anything other than perfect.' Sebastian raised her hand to his lips and watched the wild rose colour heighten the brilliance of her eyes, saw the erratic pulse beat at the base of her slender white throat just above the slender gold chain, and stopped fighting.

He would give her sapphires to match the beauty of those endlessly fascinating, dark-fringed eyes, fasten them around her neck, her wrists, find diamonds worthy of gracing her fingers. Rosie, who had never asked or expected anything of him, would be lavished with everything great wealth could buy. She would be his woman.

His taut body surged. The wooing had only just begun. He had been a blind fool to fight against what she could do to him, to deprive himself of the ecstasy that was in her power alone to give him.

If she wanted him.

His heart crashed against his ribs. She'd been a virgin. She wasn't promiscuous. That had to mean their night of wild passion had meant something to her, that it hadn't just been a lusty itch that had needed to be scratched. Had to!

A pulse beat at his temples. He had to know. He lifted her cool hand and brought it to the side of his face and had his answer.

She moved closer. He could feel the fine tremors that raced through her slender frame. Her lush mouth was parted, soft and full, slick and moist. Her trapped hand gently unfurled, her long fingers lying against the hard plane of his face, the other lifting, shyly following the shape of his mouth.

Sebastian hauled in an aching breath when she raised desire-drowned eyes to his. She was his! He had her! Life had never tasted as sweet!

Blood thundered in his ears, deafening him. He dipped his dark head to plunder her mouth with his own but a movement in his peripheral vision stopped him.

He smothered a savage oath. The young waiter cleared his throat impassively and smoothly advanced, placing the champagne in its bucket of ice on the table set before one of the tall windows. He opened the bottle deftly, replaced it in the cooler. 'Five minutes, sir?'

'Thank you.' Sebastian didn't know how he got the words out and still managed to sound in control. Hoist by his own petard, wasn't that the saying? Having the caterers around, in and out of the room, had been a way of making sure that he kept his hands off Rosie. But that had been when he'd been still fighting what he felt, still unsure. Now he wished them a million miles away.

His smile tinged with irony, he slipped an arm around Rosie's tiny waist and led her to the table. He poured the wine and handed her a foaming flute of the pale golden liquid, noting the feverish brilliance of her eyes, the way her nipples were standing proud beneath the fine gold covering, tormenting him.

Dios! How was he going to get through this evening? Gritting his teeth, he pulled out a chair for her, then sat down himself. Quickly. Using the large linen napkin to cover his lap, he hid the evidence of what she was doing to him.

Rosie gulped the cool liquid gratefully. She felt almost unbearably hot. Heated. Fire pulsing through her veins. He had been going to kiss her. Her fantasy had been changing into reality.

Her eyes on the city lights that spangled the night sky, Rosie desperately cast round for something to say to break the suddenly deafening silence. The fantasy creature, the Spaniard's golden woman who had smiled at her from the mirror earlier this evening, wouldn't be tongue-tied and all knotted up inside in this sort of situation. She'd be sparkling, relaxed, seductive and secure. And she knew she was none of these things as she heard herself blurting, 'I've never been to London before. My own capital city and I know next to nothing about it. You know loads more, and you're a foreigner!'

Her words sounded crass. Rosie flushed. Deeply disappointed by her gaucherie, she swallowed the remaining contents of her glass in one huge gulp, then prayed she wouldn't further disgrace herself by burping and vehemently vowed to kill herself if she did.

'Then one day it will be my pleasure to introduce

you to this city.' Urbanely, Sebastian refilled her flute. 'The whole tourist bit. Yes?'

Kind eyes, kind smile. Kind words to put her at her ease. Rosie knew he didn't expect her to respond. Taking him at his word would presuppose they would be meeting up in the future, on her return from Spain—or after the pregnancy issue had been settled one way or another. And they both knew that wouldn't happen.

Thankfully, the waiter appeared with the first course. Prawn and rice vinaigrette. Pushing the intrusive question of her possible pregnancy out of her head, Rosie determined to make the best of this evening, the last she would ever spend alone with him. She loved him desperately so she was entitled, wasn't she?

Through the first course he talked easily of many things, his sexily accented voice velvety and low. Rosie responded as best she could; a bit difficult because her throat kept closing up.

He'd been on the verge of kissing her; she just knew it. When the caterers had left, would he still want to kiss her then? The way he seemed unable to take his eyes off her, his main course of tender lamb chops with herb butter as barely touched as hers, told her he would.

Mental images of how willingly she would go to him, their bodies fusing as he bent his handsome dark head to take her eager lips with his, burnt gaping holes in her brain.

Her heartbeat accelerated alarmingly and her bones felt like hot, melted honey. She wanted him so badly.

The hired waiter came to remove their plates. Rosie

didn't know whether or not he raised his eyebrows at the amount of the delicious food left uneaten. Her eyes had again collided dizzily with the sizzling molten silver of Sebastian's.

She felt her heavy lids drop lower. She couldn't look away. He mesmerised her. His eyes dropped to her softly parted lips and the note of command was back in his voice as he instructed, 'You may as well clear up and call it a night, Adrian. Should we want coffee we'll fix it ourselves.'

Rosie shivered convulsively, her veins coursing with excitement. She knew now what her mother had felt for her father. She was lost in love, drawn by a force far stronger than herself, all her principles forgotten in this clamouring need for just one man.

Alone. Silence.

Rosie ran the tip of her tongue over her suddenly parched lips, the greedy starburst of excitement sending her giddy, her legs almost buckling beneath her as he reached over, clamped lean fingers around her narrow wrist and drew her to her feet.

Drew her to him, to the hard, powerful domination of his lean body, his driven groan turning her inside out as he admitted harshly. 'I have never wanted anything as much as I want you right now. You want this, too.'

The heat of his body sent her up in smoke. The palms of his hands against the bare flesh of her back, the hard evidence of his desire a shaft of dizzying, exultant excitement against the soft curve of her tummy, sent her rocketing into orbit.

Unable to lie to him, unable to verbalise an affirmative because the power of speech had deserted her,

Rosie lifted her hands to draw his head down, raising her flushed face, her lips parting to invite his kiss.

Raw passion, shocking in its intensity, had her clinging to his wide shoulders as if her life depended on it and she was shaking all over, gasping for air, when he lifted his head, his eyes glittering, and told her jaggedly, 'You are sensational, *cara mia.* Do you know that? You reach me as no other woman ever has.'

On a tide of wild emotion, Rosie took his words and held them deep inside her heart, imprinted them indelibly on her brain.

Her experience of men was about enough to be engraved on the head of a very small pin, and he might be shooting an often-used line, but he sounded really sincere, and just for this magical night she needed to believe him. And willingly she consigned all power of thought to blissful oblivion when his hands drifted upwards, over her bare arms, her shoulders, fire trailing in their wake, as he found the catch that held the halter straps of her dress in place and released it, drawing the soft fabric down to expose her tingling, aching breasts.

His intent gaze sparked a savage ache deep in her pelvis and she clung to him, barely able to stand, as his driven voice told her, 'I want to look at you. All of you.' His deft fingers found the tiny concealed zip where the gold tissue ended just above her waistline, tugged it down and allowed the dress to pool at her feet.

A convulsive shudder crashed through her as he knelt in front of her, his hands sliding over the feminine curve of her hips, his dark head bent as his mouth homed in on the blonde curls at the apex of her quivering thighs, separated from the heat of his questing lips by the thin barrier of her lacy briefs.

Throwing her head back, her fingers convulsing in his soft dark hair, a strangled groan of tumultuous, feverish ecstasy was wrenched from her. Lifting her pelvis, drawn by an instinct as old as time, Rosie shifted her feet and parted her legs.

'Perfección!' Sebastian whispered the word aloud. Rosie was curled around him, her soft fine hair spread out on the pillow. He couldn't stop looking at her and his heart was bursting with so much tenderness he thought it might explode.

She had slept for a little while. Half an hour, no longer, but by the amber glow of the single bedside lamp he could see she was beginning to wake, the thick twin crescents of her lashes stirring against her fine, slightly flushed skin.

His heart twisted with a happiness he could barely contain. He had found what he'd previously cynically believed to be an entirely mythical creature: a woman he could trust with his life, adorable, trusting, incredibly sexy, open and generous in her lovemaking. A woman without a devious or greedy bone in her beautiful body.

Gently tracing the kiss-swollen outline of her slightly parted lips, he willed her to wake. He needed her to wake, if only for long enough to hear what he had to say.

Throughout this never-to-be-forgotten night their lovemaking had been too tempestuous to allow for words, and the final time, just before she'd given a drowsy purr of pleasure and fallen asleep in his arms with the total grace of a felled sapling, it had been so slow and beautiful it had brought tears to his eyes.

He would ask her to be his wife. He could no longer envisage a life without her.

Putting a curb on his impatience, he slowly withdrew his fingers from the totally erotic exploration of her mouth and dropped his hand, curving it gently around one pert breast, allowing her to wake naturally.

Rosie couldn't feign sleep for a single moment longer. How could she when the peaking of her breast as it surged into his hand was a dead giveaway? Her conscience, always such a drag according to her former classmates, was giving her hell.

Whatever happened, she would love this man to the end of her days. She had to be honest with him, she thought emotionally. No more hiding behind half-truths and evasions. He might hate her for what she was going to have to tell him, but it was a risk she was going to have to take.

Her eyes opened unwillingly and met his. She tugged in a sharp huff of breath. Propped up on one elbow, he was leaning over her. His mouth curved in a smile, and if that wasn't blind adoration on his lethally handsome face then the light, or her wishful imagination, had to be playing tricks on her.

'*Querida*—' The throaty catch in his voice made her almost lose her nerve, abandon herself to the glistening intent in his eyes.

But, 'I have to tell you something.' She reached up to place a warning finger across his mouth, then hastily withdrew it when he laved it with his tongue. Out with it, she reminded herself sternly, and dragged herself up against the pillows, pulling her knees right up under her chin, unconsciously making the smallest possible target for the distaste that would surely follow.

Her voice rasping as she did her utmost to school out the slightest unsteadiness, she admitted, 'I should have told you before. I am Sir Marcus's illegitimate daughter.'

CHAPTER EIGHT

A HEAVY heartbeat of breathless silence. Rosie felt like bursting into tears. He didn't have to say a word. She knew he had gone from her, retreated behind the bleak façade he seemed able to summon at will. It hurt horribly and, too late, she wished the words unsaid.

Sebastian swung his long legs off the bed, located his towelling robe and shrugged his shoulders into it. Tying the belt around his waist, he turned to face her and said flatly, 'I don't believe you.'

His perfect woman was as flawed as all the rest. He had no idea what kind of devious game she was playing, but, by all that was holy, he knew Marcus had adored his wife—his own wonderful, loving Tia Lucia.

Marcus had devoted his life to his invalid wife, caring for her to the end of her days. He could not, would not, believe him capable of straying, much less of getting his mistress with child and casually abandoning her—which was what Rosie had to be implying if what she had let slip about her mother's single status and financial struggles could be believed.

If he could believe anything she said!

'I'm sorry, but it's true.'

Her voice was thick with unshed tears and her eyes were anguished. She could easily convince a more gullible man, he thought, his breath shortening, his mouth flattening. She was a pretty fair actor, he granted her that. Hiding behind that air of injured innocence. Well, it took one to know one—he was just as successfully hiding the savagely painful blow she had dealt him.

Turning sharply, he strode across the room to press the overhead light switch. He needed to see her more clearly, read what was going on inside her beautiful lying head.

In the few seconds while his back had been turned she'd dragged the coverlet up to her chin. A bit late to modestly hide her nakedness, considering the wild intimacies of the past few hours, he decided sardonically. Then he saw the tears that were now flooding and said more gently than he'd intended, 'I don't know what you hope to gain by claiming my godfather got your mother pregnant and then apparently washed his hands of her and you. A slice of the good life? Is that what you think you can get? For that you'd need proof. Yes? Your mother is no longer here to provide it, so it's up to you. Presumably you wouldn't be making such an outlandish claim if you hadn't cooked up something to back your story up.'

He turned away. Some weak part of him couldn't stand to see her crying, the silent tears streaming unchecked against the sudden pallor of her skin. 'I'm going to take a shower,' he told her heavily. 'That gives you five minutes to decide how you're going to convince me. And I warn you, it won't be easy. You're out for what you can get, aren't you?' he stated bitterly. 'Convince Marcus you're his long lost daughter and sit back and wait for your healthy inheritance. In your dreams, Rosie. It's not going to happen. I won't let it!'

Watching him stride into the *en suite* bathroom, firmly closing the door behind him, Rosie felt her heart break. The beautiful fairytale she'd been part of ever since she'd joined him for dinner the evening before had turned into a black tragedy.

She loved him to pieces and he thought she was scum! Immediately marking her down as a lying con artist cooking up an evil scheme to somehow convince a wealthy man that she was his flesh and blood just so she could get her hands on a whole load of money! So much for her silly romantic dreams!

Scrubbing her wet cheeks with the sheet, she sniffed inelegantly. She'd never gone so far as to hope he could ever love her; she wasn't completely crazy. Men like him didn't fall in love with the likes of her. But she had dreamed of fondness and affection, of a warmth in his memory of her, a tenderness for the gift of her love.

As if!

To him she'd just been a good lay, she decided with rare crudeness. Good sex when he'd wanted it, paid for with a bunch of fancy clothes!

Sliding off the bed, she stalked back to her room. Five minutes to 'cook something up'! She could give him all the proof he needed in less than five seconds!

Well, he could wait, she decided furiously, swallowing tears and stoking up anger as she scrambled into her jeans and jumper, extracting all the proof she needed from the bottom of her suitcase and stuffing it firmly into a pocket of her anorak and walking out of the door.

Two hours later she walked back in. Cooler now, calmer, that rare flash of blistering temper smoothed over by lots of brisk walking, a cup of strong black coffee and a visit to a chemist.

She'd been severely tempted to stay away longer, to wait until he would have been on his way to the airport. But, besides being cowardly, it wouldn't have been practical. His apartment would be locked up and she needed to collect the despised and shabby old clothes she'd brought with her. He could do what he liked with the stuff he'd bought; she didn't want it.

As the lift deposited her into the vestibule Sebastian shot out of the interior door. Her stomach took a nosedive. He looked absolutely furious.

'Where the hell have you been?' If his eyes were hard, his mouth was harder. He was probably within an inch of shaking the life out of her, she decided, not caring. He couldn't scare her. She wouldn't let him. She wasn't his prisoner; she could go where she pleased.

Lifting one shoulder, she told him, 'Out,' and walked past him, into the huge living area. And he followed her, of course he did, six foot plus of shimmering anger clad in a lightweight business suit. 'Buying this,' she explained without inflection, dropping the pregnancy kit on one of the low tables.

Turning, she faced him. Those lean, hard features were carved from stone, but the intense fury in his eyes might have had her running for cover if she really let herself think about it. But throughout their short and strange relationship he had called all the shots. Not any longer. Things were about to change.

'We need it, remember?' How cold her voice. She

didn't know how she managed it. Except, of course, something inside her had died when he'd accused her of being a liar and con artist, out to get her hands on Sir Marcus Troone's fortune. 'Depending on the result, you can either breathe a huge sigh of relief or do a runner. As your sainted godfather did, for all I know.'

She only had her mother's word that Marcus Troone had never known about her existence. Her mother had been a gentle, loving soul who would never do or say a thing to hurt another human being. She could have easily said that to protect the reputation of the man she had loved for all of her adult life and to stop her adored daughter from knowing that her father had turned his back on her and coldly washed his hands of all responsibility.

Now she would never know the truth of it.

'Is that what you think of me?' Sebastian demanded harshly, cold eyes raking her pale, set features.

Rosie shrugged. 'How would I know? I thought I knew what kind of man you are, but I don't.'

She thought she saw a flicker of something—discomfiture?—pass over his face. Or it might have been pain. She couldn't be sure and wasn't interested, in any case. A few hours ago she might have woven a whole load of fantasies about whatever that fleeting look had meant, translated it into regret and contrition. Not any more, though.

She dug into the pocket of her anorak. Best get it over with. And if he tried to apologise for his rock-bottom opinion of her she wouldn't listen. He had hurt her too much.

'You wanted proof.' She held out the a-bit-battered, a-bit-bulgy brown envelope. 'It's right here. Proof of the affair between my mother and Sir Marcus.' She refused to flinch away from his frowning eyes as his long fingers closed over the offering, adding acidly, 'Of course, I probably cooked it up. I'm clever like that. Stole one of the items and forged the other. Or it could be genuine. Feel free to choose.'

'Don't!' His silver eyes had somehow darkened to deepest charcoal. 'I overreacted to what you said, I admit that.' *Santo Dios!* He'd been going out of his mind these last couple of hours, starting to believe she'd taken off, that he'd never see her again, have the chance to apologise for his initial reaction.

He had always prided himself on being a good judge of character. When he'd got over the shock of what she'd claimed he'd had to admit that Rosie was no devious, manipulative, greedy bitch. He'd been the target of that particular breed enough times to recognise one when he saw one.

He pulled in a harsh breath and said in a raw undertone, 'No matter how misguided your belief that Marcus is your father, I'm sure your reasons for it are genuine but mistaken.' He stiffened his shoulders, his proud head high. 'But for my part, Rosie, please understand that I have known Marcus all of my life. I know him to be an honourable man who loved his wife. And if—and it's a big if—if he did play away from home and got some woman pregnant, he wouldn't have shied away from his responsibilities. I just can't believe that of him.'

'Some woman'!

That was her mother he was talking about!

And if that was supposed to be an apology for accusing her of being up to no good, he could forget it! She was trembling with outrage. The emotional anger she thought she'd walked out of her system flooding right back, she watched him open the envelope with a sense of bitter triumph. If he could talk himself out of that little lot then he'd missed his vocation. He should have been a politician!

Shooting her a searching look as his fingers closed around something wrapped in tissue paper, Sebastian sighed. He hadn't got through to her. She looked as if she hated him. He couldn't, in all conscience, blame her. He had gone off at half-cock, by virtue of his cynical view of most of womankind, not stopping to think until after the damage had been well and truly done. He didn't know if he'd ever be able to forgive himself for that.

As he revealed the pendant in all its harsh, glittering beauty, Rosie saw his face whiten. He glanced from it to her, his dark brows lowered. 'How did you get this?'

It was easily recognisable. A family piece. He had never seen the jewel but there had been a portrait of his aunt, as a young and vibrantly beautiful bride, hanging in the main sitting room at Troone Manor. She'd been wearing the pendant.

Years later, shortly before his aunt's death, he'd remarked on the portrait's disappearance. Marcus had told him resignedly, 'Lucia asked me to take it down. She can't bear the reminder of how she was, and how she is now.'

Swallowing the flip retort that she must have stolen it, mustn't she? Rosie answered his question levelly.

'Marcus gave it to my mother. He wanted her to have it. Just before she died she gave it to me. I didn't want it then and I don't want it now. I was going to return it when I finally got to meet him. You can do it for me.'

No answer to that, just a bleakly unreadable look before he extracted the sheet of paper. As his eyes narrowed, scanning the strong slanting script, Rosie explained without the slightest trace of emotion in her clear voice, 'Mum never named my father, but after she died I found that. I knew his identity then.'

Written on Tróone Manor headed paper it started, *My darling Molly*, and ended, *I love you always, Marcus*. And, in between, the details of a forthcoming assignation. A two-nights booking at a small coastal hotel with the information that, *We won't be known there, it's right off the beaten track, we can be together, my angel, and treasure every precious moment.*

When he finally looked at her his mouth was grim. With extreme care he refolded the letter and slotted it and the jewel back into the envelope. Pinning her with his cold eyes, he ordered, 'Get changed. We leave for the airport in less than an hour.'

Pompous, autocratic louse! 'No,' Rosie shot back at him with a definite crack in her voice now. 'I've changed my mind. I'm not going with you!'

Did he really expect her to after what he'd accused her of? So, OK, he had made a roundabout apology, and after seeing the evidence he would have to concede that her claim had some validity—unless it could be proved that her mother had been a promiscuous tramp, which she damn well hadn't been!

But his swift and humiliating change of attitude after that long night of lovemaking had left her feeling utterly besmirched and it was something she wouldn't forget in a hurry. It had clearly shown her that he cared nothing for her and had just been using her for sex because she was handy. And randy. Better to part from him right now, forget all about ever meeting her father, and put the whole tangled mess behind her.

'You come with me, whether you like it or not.' He was slotting the envelope into an inner pocket of his suit jacket. His voice might have softened but Rosie knew he was still bitingly, furiously angry. It was there in his eyes.

He couldn't make her. But even as she pointed that out to herself she knew she was in grave danger of losing control of the situation. Snatching at the only subject that could make him change his mind, she knotted her hands together and gabbled earnestly, 'You're thinking I might be having your baby, aren't you? Please don't worry. I bought that kit, didn't I? We can find out in a matter of minutes—I already read the instructions.'

Her face went fiercely scarlet. If she hadn't conceived that first time, she might have done last night. He hadn't used any protection that she'd been aware of! So much for learning by past mistakes! The test could not be able to give an accurate result this soon. Oh, why was she so unclued-up?

He looked as if he was about to say something really cutting, but all he came out with was, 'Forget the test. The results, either way, won't change a thing.'

And what the heck was that supposed to mean? She was about to ask him when his eyes suddenly softened, his warm silver gleaming into her wide, anxious blue, and she forgot her question, melting helplessly because those eyes were reminding her of the most wonderful intimacies—

Reaching her in one long stride, he put his hands on her shoulders and swung her round. 'Time to change. Go.' A tiny shove propelled her forwards, despite all her efforts to dig her heels into the carpet, his, 'You have every right to meet Marcus. I want to be around when you do. This situation has to be resolved,' ringing in her burning ears.

He could be right, she wearily admitted as she made it to the bedroom she'd been using. Unresolved, she would always wonder. Wonder what her father was like as a person, wonder if he would accept the relationship or throw her out of the door because he didn't want to be reminded of a past indiscretion he had probably long since wiped out of his memory.

And strangely, since falling in love with Sebastian, she didn't blame her father too much for what he had done. Wasn't the average man primitively programmed to cast his sexual favours far and wide to ensure his genes had the best chance of surviving, constitutionally unable to resist temptation?

If her poor besotted mother had behaved as she herself had done with Sebastian then Marcus wouldn't have stood a chance.

So, no, she no longer felt in danger of whacking him with her handbag, she decided as she changed into her cream cashmere suit with no enthusiasm at all, threw her old clothes out of her suitcase and replaced them with this and that from the lavish choice of garments Sebastian had gifted her. Then trudged out to present herself and her subdued face to the impatiently striding male she now realised she loved and hated in equal measure.

Hatred was simmering uppermost as Rosie buckled her seat belt when the plane began its descent. He hadn't spoken one word to her during the flight. Not one single word that really counted!

He'd drawn a sheaf of closely typed papers from his briefcase as soon as they'd been seated and that had been that. She might not have existed. And when, feeling really resentful by that time, she'd poked him in the ribs to get his attention, the implacably hard look he'd turned on her, the rasp in his voice as he'd asked her what she wanted, had had her muttering, 'Nothing', and flopping back in her seat, doing her best not to cry and embarrass herself.

Didn't he know how truly awful she was feeling? Didn't he care? Obviously not. All knotted up with nerves over the prospect of at last meeting her father and feeling physically ill because she'd worked out why Sebastian was still too angry to do anything other than ignore her.

Having sex with the temporary cleaning lady had been fine by him. An anonymous creature he could do his Pygmalion act on, sort out the awkward possible pregnancy problem and then wave goodbye with a clear conscience because he'd bought her a load of fancy clothes.

But having a very good idea that she was a nasty stain on his precious godfather's family escutcheon, something the family would rather not speak of in polite company, changed everything.

The warmth hit her as they walked out of the small terminal: a pleasant shock to the system after the chilly English spring. A big black car was drawn up on the tarmac, a uniformed driver walking towards them. Rosie wanted to take to her heels, run as fast and as far as she could. Her stomach churned sickeningly.

Nothing short of sheer panic would have made her forget he would rather not be reminded of her unmentionable presence, so it had to be panic that had her grasping his arm, her fingers digging into the hard muscle and bone, her voice verging on the hysterical. 'I want to go home! I can't do this! My—Marcus won't want a nasty secret from his past popping up in his life! I can't go through with this, honestly I can't!'

'Yes, you can,' Sebastian contradicted firmly, his voice deep and low. 'You can't start something as serious as this and then run away from it. I thought you had more backbone,' he added disparagingly, then broke off to greet the driver in his own language.

Stinging under his rebuke, Rosie felt her soft mouth wobble. Backbone, what backbone? Her spine had disintegrated and she felt all weak and floppy, as if her legs would give way under her at any moment.

'Come,' Sebastian commanded, unpicking her fingers from his arm and placing his hand in the small of her back, propelling her towards the waiting car where the driver was loading their luggage into the boot. 'It is not far to the *quinta*. You'll feel better when you've changed into something cooler and had a chance to relax. My mother will help put you at your ease.'

He had the rear door open, his hand still burning against her back. Instinctively, Rosie resisted. Committing herself into this car would mean committing herself to heaven only knew what kind of mayhem.

She wanted to fling herself on to Sebastian's mercy and weakly beg him to save her! Oh, how she wished she'd kept her mouth shut this morning!

Being open and honest obviously didn't always pay. They could have been here together, still in her fantasy, with him liking her and looking at her as if he found her the most desirable woman on the planet. And she could have taken her time, got to know her father before she decided whether to toss him her bombshell. Now that decision was out of her hands.

'Get in.' The grit in his voice told her he thought she was enough to try the patience of a really saintly saint, and it was still there as he added, inclining his savagely displeased and far too handsome face towards the driver, who was settling himself into his seat, 'If it helps, Tomas tells me he drove Marcus to the Cadiz office this morning. He won't be picking him up until later. You'll have time to calm down and start behaving sensibly before you get to meet him.'

An extra firmness of that inescapable hand and all the fight drained out of her. Victimised by her own big mouth, she fumbled her way into the car and sat like a sack while he walked round to the other side, opened the door and joined her.

As the big car pulled away Rosie's heart rattled against her breastbone. Now there really was no way out. And the speed with which they eventually zoomed round the outskirts of Jerez made her stomach twist itself into tight knots.

And then they were in open countryside, arid-looking plains punctuated by fertile valleys, squat white-painted farmhouses among groves of trees. Never far from the sea. Rosie tried to concentrate on the Andalucian scenery but she couldn't get past the nerve-shredding prospect of coming face to face with her father. And even worse than that was the way the man who had made such unforgettable love to her, making her feel so desired, so special, was now treating her like a pariah.

When the car swept down a narrowing road into one of the valleys where a village clustered and swept halfway up the far hillside Sebastian leaned forward and spoke to the driver.

'You look very pale,' he explained as the car slowed to a stop outside a small white house which boasted an awning, an orange tree, a chicken scratching in the dust and a few metal tables and chairs. 'Maybe a long cold drink will help.'

Rosie doubted it. Nothing but a magic wand could help her now. But she'd gratefully fall in with anything that could delay their arrival, she thought wretchedly, pushing a hank of hair away from her sweaty forehead with the back of a shaky hand.

'You could take your jacket off,' he remarked with hateful masculine superiority when he'd given his order to a short fat lady clad all in black who had pounced on their arrival as rapidly as if they were the only people to patronise her establishment in a hundred years. 'That suit's far too warm for this climate. The jacket's not welded on to your back.'

He spoke as if she were a sandwich short of a picnic! A sharp spike of resentment gave her the energy to snap back at him, 'I can't, can I? I'm not wearing anything underneath!'

Not strictly true. She was wearing one of the delicate lacy bras he'd had delivered to his apartment with all the other stuff. But mentioning underwear in this present hateful situation seemed far too intimate.

But intimacy invaded his eyes and honeyed his tongue as he drawled, his slightly accented velvety voice sending shivers down her spine, 'That prospect has much appeal. But you are right. I would not want any other eyes but mine feasting on your loveliness.'

Rosie's mind was in a dizzying whirl as the fat lady approached with two tall glasses of orange juice. What was going on here? What was he doing? Why had he brought the sex thing up again when she was trying her hardest to cope with the undisputed fact that, ever since she'd opened her mouth about her relationship with his so-honourable godfather, he'd been angry with her and disgusted by her?

When they were alone again at the small metal table she was still feeling horribly confused. If what they'd had was over—as his whole attitude had clearly shown it was as far as he was concerned—then why say things calculated to make her go weak at the knees? Did he really want to torment her? Was he that cruel?

'Drink your juice; it will help to cool you.'

The stab of impatience in his voice startled her back into the reality of why he'd broken their journey.

Rosie sat up very straight and picked up her glass. Condensation was forming on the outside and the freshly squeezed juice slid like icy cold nectar down her throat, and when he drawled, 'I take it you answered the advertisement for the temporary cleaning post because you thought you would get to meet Marcus,' she choked.

When her spluttering fit was over Sebastian took a fresh white handkerchief from his breast pocket and handed it to her. 'Well? That was your only reason for being there, wasn't it?'

He wasn't going to let up on the pressure, she thought resignedly as she mopped her face, and it got worse, really humiliating, when he added, 'And you weren't looking for something to read on the night of your birthday. You were snooping.'

Rosie tugged in a stricken breath. He was spot-on and he made her feel low-down and sneaky. Uncomfortably aware that some response was required, she nodded her bright head and started tying the handkerchief he had loaned her into knots.

Risking a rapid glance to see how he had received her affirmation, she noted that the eyes that were brittly trained on her were like shards of ice, and she knew an almost uncontrollable need to crawl under the shelter of the table and hide.

'I can understand why you didn't take me into your confidence at that time. You scarcely knew me. But after—' he allowed a pause, to punch home the shaming fact that, scarcely knowing him, she had jumped into bed with him '—after we became close you could have told me why you were there.'

Close. Did his mind only work on the sexual level

where she was concerned? Of course it did. 'We were only close in the physical sense,' she mumbled, blushing like fury. 'In every other way we're miles apart.'

'Really?' Bitter?

'Of course.' Not bitterness. Probably sarcasm. What could he possibly have to be bitter about in that context? 'A cleaning woman brought up on a sink estate, and someone like you who has never had to worry about mundane things like how to pay the gas bill.' Another knot in the soggy handkerchief. 'We're not remotely close in anything that matters. But the real reason I didn't say anything was because I didn't want to upset you,' she explained, her conscience pricking her into confessing. 'You obviously thought the world of your aunt. And you'd have been sickened if I'd told you your aunt had been betrayed and the result had been me. I just knew you'd despise what I was. A nasty stain on your family.

'And I wasn't going to do anything horrible, like blackmailing him into paying up for all those years of neglect,' she said in breathy self-defence. 'I just wanted to find out what kind of man my father was. If I liked him I would have told him who I was and that my mother had passed on and had never stopped loving him. Given him the pendant back and vanished. If I hadn't liked him I would have sent the wretched thing back anonymously.'

'Yet you did tell me, in the end,' he pointed out with supreme dryness, ignoring the greater part of her gabbled speech. 'Why?'

Rosie wriggled on her seat. He asked the most awkward questions in the coolest of voices. How could she possibly tell him she had fallen in love with him and couldn't bear to go on deceiving him?

Ignoring the love bit, she hunched her slender shoulders and managed to mutter, as if it were something to be ashamed of, 'I didn't want secrets.'

His brilliant eyes had narrowed, but his smile was something else. He simply said, 'Ah, I see,' but he looked like a man who'd just been told he'd won the lottery.

Rosie's breathing went on hold, and when he stood and said, 'Let's go face the music, shall we?' she could only scramble to her feet and follow, knowing she would never understand him in a trillion years.

Knowing, sadly, that she would never be given the opportunity to try.

CHAPTER NINE

'WELCOME to my home, Rosie. My son has told me so much about you.'

Doña Elvira looked genuinely pleased to see her and Rosie, nervously returning the older woman's smile, flicked Sebastian a puzzled sidelong glance.

'I do know how to use a telephone,' he supplied drily, and Rosie returned her attention to his mother. Of course, he would have had to let his parent know he would be arriving with a guest. Stupid of her to have imagined she would have come as an awkward surprise.

'Paquita will take your suitcases to your room, but before you freshen up after your journey Carlota is bringing cold drinks. I always find that travelling gives me the most enormous thirst. My dear husband used to say that I couldn't have been a camel in a former life!' The dark eyes sparkled as she motioned Rosie to a chair. 'Sebastian can go and winkle Terrina out from wherever she is hiding—by the pool, I think, *hijo*—and leave me to talk to Rosie; I want to get to know all about her.'

Oh, no, you don't! Rosie muttered inside her head, but the first real smile of the day brightened her features as she sank into the elegant, brocade-covered chair. Sebastian had been right about one thing: his mother—with her warm smile, her charm and slender elegance—could put the guillotine-bound occupants of a tumbril at their ease with no trouble at all.

As they had approached the house, awe had been added to her nervous trepidation. The white walls, arches and intricate ironwork and towers gave it the look of a Moorish fortress. Some house!

Her knees had knocked alarmingly as Sebastian had escorted her through a spacious colonnaded courtyard, too preoccupied to actually see the beauty of the ancient stone fountain, the flowering perfumed vines that clung to the high walls. She'd felt as out of place as a hamburger at a Lord Mayor's banquet. But Doña Elvira had immediately put her at her ease, and just for a few moments she was determined to make the most of a state of affairs that was bound to be short-lived.

'*Momento*, Mama. Terrina can wait.' She would have to, Sebastian thought grittily. Other things had taken precedence over the need to send the gold-digger packing. 'How is Marcus?' His godfather and partner had collapsed from the strain of overwork at the turn of the year, and before he was presented with his illegitimate daughter—and his own anger at the older man's dereliction of responsibility—he needed to know that he was strong enough to take it. Despite the growing certainty that Marcus had behaved dishonourably all those years ago, he still held him in high affection.

'Fighting fit.' Doña Elvira smiled an acknowledgement as a young maid carried in a tray of the promised cool drinks. 'He insists he can't wait to get back into harness and visits the Cadiz office most days.' She rose gracefully to pour from the jug of iced fruit juice. 'Needless to say, that doesn't please Terrina. She would far rather he took her shopping.'

Glass in hand, she paused. 'From observation, I would say that he's beginning to have many second thoughts in that direction. You and I saw through her, but—' She gave an eloquent shrug and carried the glass to Rosie, apologising, 'Forgive me. Prattling on about family concerns that can be of no interest to you.'

She was wrong there, Rosie thought, taking the glass. Her own feelings about Marcus's marital intentions had been ambiguous to say the least. On the one hand, she had nothing against people taking a second chance of happiness. On the other, there was the hard, resentful little feeling that, after his wife's death, he might have tracked her mother down. That he hadn't done any such thing reinforced her opinion that Molly Lambert had been just a casual secret fling. Men in his position didn't marry beneath them.

As the carved wooden door closed behind Doña Elvira, Rosie looked round the rooms she'd been given and gave a soft sigh of relief. A whole suite of rooms, combining luxury and taste, bowls of fresh flowers to perfume the air, and one set of windows to look out on to an inner courtyard and another set to give her views of the surrounding countryside and a glimpse of the distant sea. She wasn't expected to surface for another two hours, when dinner was due to be served. After Sebastian had been called away to the phone, her chat with his mother had been really calming.

With skill and a huge dose of charm the older

woman had drawn all sorts of things out of her. Her humble origins, the reason she'd had to give up her place at university where she'd intended to read sociology. The dilemma she now faced: should she try for another place and take out a student loan or continue to work for Jean to fund evening classes at the local college and end up as a secretary?

'I'm quite sure all that will take care of itself,' Doña Elvira had murmured, covering Rosie's hand with her own. 'You will see.'

Nice thought. Rosie gave a wry smile. But life didn't work like that, did it? If you left everything to fate, as the older woman had seemed to be suggesting, then nothing would ever get done, would it?

Thankfully, she removed her warm jacket and didn't have time to put it back on again as Sebastian walked in after the briefest of raps.

Instinctively, she folded her arms over her breasts. His brilliant eyes gleamed. 'I have seen you wearing much less. But I like it when you blush. However—' he moved towards her and placed his hands on her shoulders '—I know how nervous you are. I have forced you into a situation not of your liking. I have made decisions for you.' His eyes probed her flushed face, and Rosie had the strongest urge to fling her arms around him and tell him not to worry; it didn't matter. She would face whatever had to be faced if he could stop being angry with her.

'The matter does have to be resolved. But not tonight. Tomorrow will be soon enough, when you are more rested. So tonight you may eat your dinner without fear of terminal indigestion!'

Rosie's legs decided to turn into water and her

tummy flipped right over. When he smiled like that she went into emotional melt-down. She trembled, every nerve-ending leaping with wicked response to this achingly gorgeous man, but he merely touched her lips briefly with his own, then gave her a shuttered look, swung round and exited the room like a man with a pack of demons on his heels.

Refusing to let herself get into a mental tangle by trying to work out what went on in his mind to provoke such contradictory behaviour, she went through the motions of undressing and drawing a bath. But half an hour spent in a marble tub that was almost big enough to swim in, admiring the mirrored walls, the green marble floor and the exotic pot plants, produced a mood of calm acceptance.

She wouldn't be here long enough to get used to such luxury. After she'd been sprung on Marcus she'd be put on the first flight home. He couldn't kill her for being his unwanted daughter! And, as for Sebastian, it was time she started thinking like an adult woman instead of a love-struck teenager.

All he was probably used to was sex for the sake of it with any woman who was willing and took his fickle fancy. He would run far more than the proverbial mile if he discovered she had fallen in love with him.

And as long as she kept that firmly in mind she'd be all right. Get over it. Get on with her life. And, if she did turn out to be pregnant, she'd cross that bridge when she came to it.

Not wanting to dwell on that tricky subject and get herself more wound up than she already was, she hauled herself out of the bath and, wrapped in one of the huge bath sheets, padded through into the bedroom.

And stopped short, her huge eyes filled with enquiry as the woman who'd been staring out of one of the windows turned towards her.

'I did knock but you can't have heard me. So I came in to wait. You don't mind? Terrina Dysart—' She walked forward as she smilingly introduced herself. 'Marcus's fiancée. I was told you'd arrived and I did so want to meet with you.'

Clutching her towel, Rosie took the outstretched hand and returned a smile. So this was the woman her father was planning to marry. She was lovely, glossy as a catwalk model, beautifully packaged in a flame-coloured shift, the chestnut hair—commonly described as big—artfully arranged around her shoulders. Rosie felt quite pallid by comparison.

'So—' The scarlet smile widened, showing teeth as even and white and perfect as a toothpaste advertisement. 'You are Sebastian's lady. I approve! It is time he settled down.'

If only! Rosie felt a regrettable juvenile blush spreading all over her body. Is that what they all thought, that she was the Spaniard's woman? Impossible to explain who she really was and why she was here at this stage, before tomorrow morning's confrontation with Marcus.

Thankfully, Terrina didn't appear to expect a confirmation of her statement. She settled gracefully on to a silk-covered chaise and opined, 'It's just a duty visit, I suppose? You and Sebastian won't be staying long—it gets pretty boring after a while. I'm hoping to persuade Marcus to take me to Milan to shop for a trousseau.'

'That sounds fun.' Rosie hoped that was the right thing to say. She felt like a lemon, standing here wrapped in a towel, trying to make light conversation with the woman Marcus was to marry, her eyes prickling with tears because she couldn't help thinking of her mother.

If Terrina was the type her father admired, then what had he been doing with someone like Molly Lambert, the unsophisticated gardener's daughter, who had liked nothing better than grubbing about in the soil, helping things to grow?

'I ought to get dressed for dinner.' Rosie felt it was time to make an effort to show she was in control of something. 'Doña Elvira said my case had been brought here, but I can't see it.'

'Paquita will have unpacked for you.' Terrina rose to her feet and swayed over to an enormous walk-in wardrobe. 'Problem solved!' She riffled amongst the hangers, exclaiming, 'Classy! I must say, you do have fabulous taste. Go for this—' She held out a smoky-grey knee-length sleeveless chiffon dress with a discreetly plunging neckline. 'You will look perfect—a lovely foil for my orange thing!' She wrinkled her narrow nose. 'I tend to go for look-at-me colours. I'll have to learn to be more decorous when I'm the lady of the manor!'

The sudden flicker of uncertainty in the long brown eyes had Rosie quickly asserting, 'You mustn't think like that. I think you look fantastic. You are what you are. You shouldn't try to change a single thing.'

Sebastian had tried to change her, tried to turn a

sow's ear into a silk purse. And just look where it had got her. Nowhere!

'Really?' The brown eyes widened.

'Yes, really,' Rosie affirmed as she took the selected dress. 'Now, I must get changed or I'm bound to be late. I'll see you at dinner?'

'Of course.' Terrina made a move to leave, then hesitated. 'I—oh, dammit! Look, do you mind if I'm frank?' The pampered hands with their long, painted fingernails were twisting together. 'Could you get Sebastian to leave as soon as possible? Tell him you'd like to go to Seville, or something? He's a lovely man, but he doesn't like me. I'm pretty sure he'll try to break me and Marcus up.'

'Why on earth would he want to do that?' Rosie soothed immediately. The other girl had obviously got her wires crossed somewhere, but she did seem genuinely troubled. Her smooth brow wrinkled. Hadn't Sebastian said that Terrina wasn't fit to touch her shoes, or something along those lines? Looking at this lovely creature, it didn't make any sense. 'And how could he not like you?' she added for good measure.

'Because—' Terrina bit down on her lower lip, then dragged in a huge breath. 'You won't like this, but it is true. As things stand, Sebastian is Marcus's heir. Everything—his fifty per cent holding in the business, his property, the millions sloshing around in bank accounts—goes to Sebastian. He stands to lose the lot if Marcus remarries. As his wife I would inherit everything.'

As Rosie's mouth fell open, the other girl said harshly, 'That's why he'd do anything to break us up.

Think about it,' and exited the room on a cloud of musky perfume, leaving Rosie gaping.

Sebastian wouldn't do a thing like that! He was wealthy enough in his own right. He was really fond of his godfather; some of the things he'd said proved that. He wouldn't try to deprive him of his future happiness with a new wife just for sordid financial gain.

And yet—Her brow wrinkled. When she'd revealed her true identity he had immediately accused her of scheming to place herself as Marcus's heir, his initial thoughts only of all that money—his own inheritance. No mention at that stage of his aunt's betrayal.... The sudden doubts made her feel sick. With an effort she pushed them away.

Terrina, for all her friendliness, had to be mentally deranged, poor thing, to even imagine that Sebastian would act that way—it was the only solution. Wasn't it?

'You look exquisite. Perfect.' Sebastian cupped her bare elbow with his hand and escorted her out of the bedroom. 'We assemble in the small *sala*, drink a glass of *fino*, make small talk and then go in to dinner. It is the ritual in my mother's home.' His voice was light, his smile warm, his compliments on her appearance a welcome boost to her self-confidence. But Rosie could feel the tension in him; it seemed to flow from him in unsettling waves.

On the point of confiding Terrina's odd misgivings, she firmly clamped her mouth shut. If she said anything at all on that subject she'd probably be accused of mischief-making. She had enough on her plate without that! In a few moments she would be introduced to her father! And the way Sebastian's tautly muscled thigh was brushing lightly against hers as they walked the length of the corridor was making her feel decidedly drunk.

But for once the physical contact didn't make her blush. In fact, her face felt all white and pinched. At the carved wooden doors Sebastian paused. He gave her an unnervingly tender glance.

'Try to relax, *cara*. No traumatic revelations this evening, remember. Just be your own natural, sweet self and put all your anxieties aside until the morning. Don't forget, I am here with you.'

As if she could forget a thing like that! Around him she was flooded with so much fierily wicked weakness she couldn't think straight. And her anxieties refused to be put aside; they just kept hammering at her brain. Nevertheless, she managed a wavery smile, told him, 'Thank you, I appreciate your support,' and steeled herself to walk through the door he'd opened for her. Head high, smile glued to her face.

It was a beautiful room with a painted, intricately plastered ceiling, tall windows, delicate furniture, a magnificent hand-painted Chinese screen.

Doña Elvira, Terrina and the man she had come so far to see.

Marcus Troone began to get to his feet, then abruptly sank back in his chair, his hands gripping the carved and gilded arms, his strong features losing every vestige of colour as he gasped, 'Molly!'

CHAPTER TEN

ROSIE'S blood ran cold, then surged with a rush of anxiety which was uncomfortably spiked with guilt. She was responsible for her father's collapse.

He'd taken one look at her and mistaken her for her mother! Hadn't Jean always said how alike they were? She should have remembered that.

Sebastian had already reached his godfather's side, and Rosie pulled herself together and sped after him. Elvira rose swiftly from her chair and tugged on the bell rope to summon one of the servants. Only Terrina stayed where she was, staring.

'Don't fuss!' Marcus grumbled as Sebastian leant over him and loosened his collar. 'I'm perfectly all right. Bit of a shock, that's all. And I don't want a doctor,' he stated strongly, picking up on Sebastian's terse instruction to Doña Elvira. 'If you send for him I shall refuse to see him!'

'Recovered, obviously,' Sebastian murmured drily as Paquita appeared, to vanish again to fetch the water Doña Elvira requested.

Angled behind Sebastian's back, Rosie hardly dared show her face in case she triggered another collapse. Or worse. How awful if something happened to him before they exchanged a single word!

But that dire event seemed extremely unlikely as Sir Marcus Troone rose smartly to his feet. Sebastian swung round, his features set, looped an arm around her waist and positioned her to face the older man.

Rosie simply stared. She couldn't help it. A still handsome man, he had altered little from the photograph she'd seen. His face a littler heavier, his waistline a little thicker. Deep blue eyes searched her pale features but his firm voice was kind as he apologised, 'I'm sorry. I don't usually greet guests by falling flat on my back! You remind me of someone I used to know.'

'Rosie—' Sebastian's voice was sharpened steel. 'Now, I think.'

Knowing exactly what he meant, her eyes appealed to his. 'Should I? Now?'

'Sí.'

'May I know what you're talking about?' Marcus's keen eyes encompassed them both as he waved aside the water Elvira held out to him. Rosie took a deep breath. She had the floor and didn't feel over the moon about it. Huge understatement!

But Sebastian was right. After he'd called out her mother's name in shock there could be no more prevarication. Besides, she tried to reassure herself, she needn't worry too much. Healthy colour had come back into his face and he looked strong as an ox. Far stronger than she felt!

Grateful for Sebastian's supportive hand on her waist, Rosie gathered her courage and said gently, before her father could explode with impatience, 'I remind you of my mother. Molly Lambert.'

The sternly sculpted mouth was suddenly unsteady. A spasm of emotion tightened his features before they relaxed into a semblance of a smile. 'Molly. Of course. Molly's child; you look exactly as I remember her.' A muscle jerked in his throat. 'I'm afraid I lost touch with her many years ago. How is she?'

Rosie swallowed. Hard. Didn't he make the connection? His adultery had led to a pregnancy. He hadn't wanted to know. Couldn't he guess who she really was? Or was he firmly into denial?

'My mother died a few months ago.' Her voice was flat. 'That's why I wanted to find you. Mum never told me who my father was, but before she died she gave me a pendant, given to her by my father—'

'We have rock-solid reasons to believe that Rosie is your daughter, Marcus,' Sebastian cut in with the voice of a man swiping through too much waffle.

Rosie's breath snagged as the colour washed out of her father's face. A film of tears dampening his eyes as he sank back into his chair, he said thickly, 'I'm so sorry Molly's gone. Too young.'

Casting Sebastian a fulminating look for jumping in with two left feet where she had meant to tread so carefully, she pulled a chair close to Marcus and took both his hands in hers.

Elvira murmured, 'Oh, my dear!' and Rosie didn't know if she had directed the remark to Marcus or to her. At the moment she didn't care. All her attention was given to the troubled man who was her long lost father.

'Please don't upset yourself,' she said softly. 'I promise I'm not here to cause trouble. As Sebastian said, there are reasons, but it's a long story and it will wait until morning.'

'Oh, pur-leese! Just get on with it!' Terrina's voice, suddenly harsh, sliced through the moment of fraught silence and, as if that had been a wake-up call, Marcus rallied, his spine straightening, his strong fingers tightening around Rosie's.

'I want you to tell me all you can about Molly,' he said urgently. 'She disappeared all those years ago. Her parents clammed up and refused point-blank to tell me where she was or why she'd gone. Even after all these years I need to know! If—if you really are my daughter—' Rosie's fingers were in danger of being crushed by the pressure he was exerting '—I have to know everything—'

Agitation couldn't be good for him, Rosie decided, and told him as gently as she could, 'Mum left her home, the village, and dropped out of college because she was pregnant with me. She wouldn't tell me who my father was, but she did tell me he was married. I guess she felt that telling you she was pregnant would cause you a whole heap of trouble, so she took the decision to disappear. But I do know,' she added quickly as a terrible spasm of pain crossed his face, 'that she loved you always. She never looked at another man. She was pretty, and she did have offers, but she just wasn't interested.'

If his eyes could still fill with moisture over a lover he'd lost almost twenty-one years ago, then his love must have been sincere and strong. Just as her mother's had been. Ready tears welled up in Rosie's eyes. It was a horribly sad story.

Marcus said heavily, his voice cracking with emotion, 'She should have told me. She needn't have had to cope on her own. We both knew I could never leave my wife, but I would have cared for Molly and my child. I would have loved you both. So much love. Gone to waste.'

'So you admit to having an adulterous affair.' Sebastian's tone was icy. He walked into Rosie's line of vision. He looked intimidating and Rosie's heart sank, landing up somewhere beneath the soles of her shoes. From what she'd been able to gather Sebastian had adored his aunt Lucia, and her husband had betrayed her in the worst possible way. If she'd kept her nose out of it, refused to follow her need-to-know instincts, then this rift would never have been created.

She felt absolutely dreadful. She had messed up, big time!

'I must alter the dinner arrangements,' Elvira said briskly. 'Trays, I think. Later. Please excuse me. Are you coming, Terrina?'

'No. I'm staying right where I am.' Rosie caught the look of scorn in the other woman's eyes and felt totally withered. Unlike Elvira, a tactful withdrawal obviously didn't come high on her list of priorities. 'If I'm to be landed with a grown up stepdaughter when I marry I need to be in on this.'

'Terrina—leave us!' Marcus ordered firmly, and Rosie felt sick. She was causing problems all round and right now she didn't like herself very much. Pulling her hands from Marcus's grip, she wrapped her arms around her body and hoped with all her might that Sebastian could eventually find it in his heart to forgive his godfather, even if he never forgave her for being the catalyst.

Not even Terrina could ignore that forceful command, and when the three of them were alone Marcus stood facing his godson, who was also his nephew by marriage, the close bond this implied seemingly on the point of shattering, judging by the coldly distant set of Sebastian's strong features, the proud angle of his dark head.

'Try not to despise me, Seb.' It was an order, not a plea. Miserably, her heart in her mouth, Rosie watched what promised to be a clash of two Titan characters. 'I loved Lucia. I would never have hurt her. But because of her condition my feelings for her of necessity became more like the love of a father for a sick child.'

'So you looked for relief, right there, practically under Lucia's nose,' Sebastian said darkly, his eyes stony.

'It happened!' Marcus shot straight back. 'Seb—I was a normal, healthy male, with normal, healthy needs. But I never even considered looking elsewhere. Until that summer when I first met Molly. Oh—' he shrugged impatiently '—I knew the Lamberts had a daughter, must have seen her about the place from time to time. But that summer, when she worked with us, it was as if I'd been struck by a bolt of lightning. It just happened. We couldn't help ourselves. We tried, by God we both tried!'

Again the impatient shrug, as if he couldn't expect anyone who hadn't experienced something similar to understand. 'We were careful—Lucia never even guessed.' He heaved a heavy sigh. 'Molly knew, and understood, that I would never leave Lucia for her. Your aunt relied on me too much, not only to arrange and oversee the twenty-four-hour nursing care she had begun to need by then, but for company, for the knowledge that someone really cared enough about her to stay with her, helping her in her fight against her cruel disease.'

'So you sacrificed your mistress and your unborn child just to keep your reputation sweet,' Sebastian injected coldly.

'Dammit, man! Haven't you been listening?'

Marcus was clearly losing his cool. Rosie wondered dizzily if she should intervene. But neither of them seemed aware of her existence any longer. She would have liked nothing better than to creep quietly away and hide somewhere but she couldn't do that.

And Marcus was grinding out, his skin reddening, 'I didn't know Molly was pregnant. Had I done I would have been over the moon about it. I always wanted a child. Molly's child—' Words seemed to fail him there, but after a moment his voice strengthened. 'Had I known, I would have settled her somewhere on the other side of the country—a cottage with a garden; she was mad about growing things—I would have supported her and our child. Something would have been discreetly arranged. But Molly vanished. At the time I believed she'd found the strength I didn't have, the strength to break the spell between us. But I had no idea of the truth. So how could I have helped? Answer me that!'

Even though Rosie's vision was blurred with tears she could see the way Sebastian's hard shoulders suddenly relaxed, see Marcus turn to her. 'But Molly gave me a daughter.' He held out a hand but Rosie ignored it. She was trying to read Sebastian's expression, to see if he understood that love could be devastating, take precedence over everything else.

She did. Since falling in love with him she understood it only too well, and could forgive both her parents for what had happened. But if Sebastian had never experienced the wild passion of that kind of love, didn't know what it could do to a person, how it could sweep normal moral considerations aside, then he would never forgive the older man.

Her wide eyes still seeking his, he swept her a long, level glance before turning to the door. His voice stiffly polite, he observed, 'I misjudged you, Marcus. I doubted your honour. Forgive me for that. As you were unaware of your lover's pregnancy you can't be blamed for doing nothing to help. Now…' he paused at the great carved doors '…you need privacy to get to know each other. I'll leave you, and make sure you're not disturbed.'

Rosie's heart seemed to swell to twice its normal size as she gazed at the spot where he had been. So that was why he'd been so simmeringly angry. Nothing to do with her at all, or only indirectly. He—as evidenced by his determination to keep her where he could see her until they knew whether or not she was pregnant—would never shirk his duty. He'd been coldly angry because he'd believed Marcus had.

At least the rift she'd caused between them had been healed, she thought thankfully, her eyes misting.

'Rosie—'

Dimly, through a haze of emotional tears, she watched Marcus walk towards her. He took her hands and drew her to her feet. 'Molly's child, my daughter,' he said brokenly. 'Such a precious gift.'

The dimly lit corridor stretched endlessly in front of her. Was this the way to her room, or wasn't it? Rosie felt wrung out with exhaustion. She wished Sebastian would appear. She needed him. Not to talk—she was all talked out—but just to be close, and if that was weak, well, she couldn't help it.

Her father had wanted to know all there was to know about her life and her mother's. She'd told him everything, skating rapidly over the bad bits so as not to add to the guilt he was obviously and wrongly feeling.

Touching on the pendant, she'd promised to return it to him in the morning, but he'd said, 'It's been in the family for decades. It's yours now, as of right. One of the greatest sadnesses of my life has been the lack of an heir, and now I have you.'

'Oh, no!' Rosie reddened with mortification. 'I don't want anything! I didn't try to find you for what I could get out of you! All I wanted to do was get to know you a little. Mum and I didn't have any relatives, not since my grandparents died.' And even they had turned their backs on them. 'Then, when Mum—went, I just wanted to feel I did sort of belong to someone.'

She was just thankful that her father was a decent man and not the callous philanderer she'd half believed he must be. That was all that really mattered to her. And Marcus had given her the most wonderful smile. 'Don't you think I don't know that? You are your mother's daughter, not a grasping bone in your body. And if you're as sensitive to others' needs as she was you'll agree to spend some time with me, back at Troone. We can really get to know each other while you decide what you want to do with your future. For the moment, that's all I ask of you.'

All in all, it had been an emotionally exhausting two or three hours, and now it was late and, stupidly, she'd got herself lost in this huge building.

There was another corridor branching off the one she'd found herself in. Perhaps that was the one that would lead to her room? Trouble was, the house was built around a series of courtyards. She could be wandering around all night!

She forced herself on. Then, her eyes widening, she heard Terrina's voice coming from a partly open door. Saying something about preferring the cheque to be made out in US dollars. Sounding fairly stroppy about it.

Never mind that—she was saved! Terrina would know how to find her room! Lurching forward on a burst of adrenalin-fuelled energy, she stumbled to a halt when she heard Sebastian's voice answering, 'If that's what you want.' A tiny pause, then, 'Take it and think yourself lucky. It should be enough to keep you in nail polish and perfume until you find another rich sucker to attach yourself to. It's nowhere near what you'd have had access to as Marcus Troone's wife, of course, but the alternative is having him throwing you out with nothing at all, should he get to hear what I could tell him. Be packed and ready to leave in the morning.'

Rosie's eyes closed in pain. She shivered in shocked disbelief. She knew she shouldn't be eavesdropping but she couldn't move.

Sebastian was blackmailing her father's fiancée! Making her break off the engagement! Because he would stop at nothing—as Terrina had as good as confided—to prevent Marcus remarrying, thus diverting his property away from him!

And Terrina's acid drawl hammered the awful fact hard into her cringing brain. 'Congratulations! You've stopped me coming between you and your inheritance. But you're not home and dry yet. You'd better get your skates on and slap a wedding ring on his new-found daughter's finger, hadn't you? It's the only way to make sure of your future inheritance.'

'Believe me—' Sebastian's voice carried a smile '—I intend to.' The sound of a chair's legs being scraped across the floor.

Both hands over her mouth, Rosie fled. She'd stumbled into the blackest of black nightmares! She might have found her father, but her heart was utterly and hopelessly shattered.

It all fell into place now. Sebastian wouldn't let anyone stand in the way of his future inheritance. He'd prevented his godfather's remarriage and now all he had to do was marry the new heir and, bingo! He'd get what he wanted.

Chillingly, she recalled his immediate reaction when she'd told him who she was. His greedy instincts had come to the fore when he'd accused her of trying to get his godfather's money. When she'd put the proof of her identity into his hands he'd backtracked a little, added all that stuff about not being able to believe the older man could have betrayed his wife, the aunt Sebastian had professed to have loved so much. And later, when he'd actually seen the proof and had had time to think, he'd asked a few more questions and had been nice to her again.

Deciding that she, and not he, would be likely to

inherit Marcus's wealth, he'd known he'd have to sweeten her up all over again, get her ready for the marriage proposal he'd admitted to Terrina he was going to make.

Louse!

CHAPTER ELEVEN

THE last thing Rosie wanted to do was face the new day. She'd finally sobbed herself to sleep, and when Paquita had woken her at ten with a breakfast tray she'd wanted nothing more than to bury her face in the pillow and tell her to go away.

But, remembering her manners, she'd thanked her anyway, ignored the tray which had been left on a small table beneath one of the long windows, and hauled herself to the adjoining bathroom, where the sight of her puffy red eyes and swollen nose hadn't done a single thing to alleviate her misery.

The discovery that she wasn't pregnant was the final blow. Though it should be one enormous relief, she sniped at herself, as she opened the doors to the hanging cupboard and dispiritedly wondered what to wear.

Was she really such a love-lorn idiot as to actually want to be carrying Sebastian's baby? She should be calling for champagne to celebrate the fact that she wasn't to be the unmarried mother of a child who bore a slimy, manipulative blackmailer's genes!

Covering up was the order of the day, she decided. She felt as if she was in mourning. For a baby who hadn't been there in the first place? For the loss of love?

Oh, snap out of it!

What she'd overheard had been a blessing in disguise—well, hadn't it? She might have spent the rest of her days mooning uselessly over a worthless, mercenary skunk, remembering…

She didn't want to remember. It made her cringe all over to even think of him! And she had found her father, and he was a good man. And that should make up for everything. Well, shouldn't it?

Stylish cotton trousers in a pale smoky blue with a matching short-sleeved jacket over a deeper blue vest was as sober as she could get, given the choice of garments she'd stuffed into her suitcase.

She would much rather be pulling on her own scuffed jeans and one of her plain, well washed T-shirts. Wearing the clothes Sebastian had bought her now made her feel kind of creepy, like the sort of woman who accepted gifts for services rendered.

She was listlessly brushing her hair when Doña Elvira entered the room. She smiled warmly. 'How are you feeling this morning?'

'Shell shocked,' Rosie admitted, laying down the brush and turning to face the other woman. That elegant lady looked sympathetic but mightily pleased at the same time. If she thought her admission had to do with at last meeting her father, and nothing to do with finding out what kind of man Sebastian was, then that was fine by Rosie.

'It must have been a deeply emotional meeting,' Doña Elvira sympathised, verifying Rosie's assumption. She probably didn't know what kind of man her precious son was, either, and Rosie wasn't about to take the blinkers off her eyes. She could keep her illusions, and welcome!

'But a happy one, yes?' the older woman insisted.

'I breakfasted with Marcus and he gave me the background details. He is like—how do you say it?—a dog with two heads!'

'Tails,' Rosie corrected automatically, and tried to smile because she knew it was expected of her.

It turned into a sigh when Sebastian's mother scolded, 'You haven't touched your breakfast. You must eat. The coffee will be cold. I will send for fresh.'

'No, really—the juice will be fine; I never touch much for breakfast.' A whopping fib—in normal circumstances she ate like a horse—and Rosie condemned herself as she resignedly obeyed the imperious gesture inviting her to sit at the small table.

Better make an effort or her hostess might guess that her lack of appetite and hang-dog expression sprang from something even more traumatic than her first meeting with her father.

While she dutifully sipped the cool fruit juice Elvira sank on to the chair opposite.

'Your father is an honourable man, Rosie. He must have loved your mother deeply to forget his marriage vows. He was so careful of Lucia right up until the end of her life. He would never have left her, and he assures me your mother accepted that. He had no idea she was pregnant with you when she left. You do believe that, don't you?'

Rosie nodded, the ever-ready tears misting her eyes. Her mother had experienced so much hardship because of the decision she'd made, but at least she'd done what she'd thought was right.

'Lucia had already lost so much.' Doña Elvira sighed. 'Marcus couldn't take her faith in him away from her. It must have been so hard for him when she fell ill so early on in their married life. They were both truly desperate to have children and, sadly, that didn't happen. But now he has you, and he's so happy about it. I tell you the truth—he can't stop smiling!'

Cue a big smile of her own. Elvira must be wondering why she looked as if she'd lost a ten-pound note and found a farthing! 'I'm happy about it, too,' she assured the other woman, and that, at least, was the whole truth.

'And Terrina's gone. Sebastian is driving her to Seville as we speak. The engagement's off, thank goodness. She wouldn't have been right for him.'

Rosie's smile faded immediately. Terrina had gone because Sebastian had threatened her. She asked anxiously, 'Is Marcus upset?'

'Not at all. I think it came as a relief to him that she called it off before he was forced to! I know he's been having second thoughts—being married to such a demanding creature would have been a high-price to pay for getting a child. Which was all he wanted from her, if the truth were to be told. And because you came to find him that space in his life is filled!'

She had come to Spain and made herself known because Sebastian had forced her hand. Because he'd known that in presenting Marcus with his own flesh and blood he would have been halfway home in his driving need to get rid of Terrina, the woman who, as Marcus's wife, would stand in the way of his inheritance?

Left to her own dithery devices she would probably have tried to make some kind of contact with her father, just to satisfy her curiosity. When that had been accomplished she would in all likelihood have removed herself from his vicinity without revealing who she was, because she would have been afraid of an outright rejection, or, even worse, of being laughed at.

So why hadn't Sebastian let her go her own way? He must have known that, in insisting that she tell her father who she was, he ran the risk of putting her between him and the inheritance he was so keen to hang on to?

Perhaps there was more to his threats to Terrina than she knew about.

She was so muddled now she was sure her head was on the verge of bursting, and when Elvira said, 'Your father is anxious to spend the day with you. I thought we might start by showing you around the house and the various courtyards,' Rosie sprang to her feet with more energy than she'd managed to find all morning, desperately anxious to put all thoughts of Sebastian out of her mind until she could speak to him and demand to know why he'd threatened Terrina.

Peace. Silence and tranquillity. Just the sound of the water playing in the courtyard's central fountain, the whisper of the breeze in the parasol pines beyond the high stone outer wall. Trailing patterns of mist were silvered in the moonlight.

Rosie breathed deeply of the soft, perfumed air. The household slept. She would never lose her way in the extensive building again. She'd been given the complete guided tour.

Not that she'd be here for much longer. Marcus

was anxious to get back to England. He wanted to introduce her to his friends, his staff, and anyone else with the slightest inclination to listen. And to show her around the home that had been in their family for hundreds of years.

When she'd confessed that she already knew Troone Manor fairly intimately—at floor and window pane level—explaining about the way she'd taken a temporary cleaning job, he'd hugged her fiercely and thanked her for taking the trouble when others in her situation might have written him off.

It had been a hectic, emotional day, one way or another. And as she and her father had taken the first steps towards getting to know one another she'd been able to stop thinking about Sebastian who had, apparently, decided to combine driving Terrina to Seville—her preferred destination—with a business meeting. He wasn't expected back until some time tomorrow.

But now her mind was filling with him. The way he held his head, the way he looked and the way he felt. The palms of her hands ached to touch his face; her lips were tremulously softening for his kiss. No matter how hard she'd tried to convince herself of his mercenary, manipulative nature, or how often she'd told herself that mourning over unrequited love was a huge waste of time, she couldn't stop thinking of him, wanting and needing him.

A solitary tear slid down her cheek, and when she heard approaching footsteps over the paving slabs she hurriedly wiped it away with the back of her hand. Her father? One of the staff?

'Querida.'

She would know that voice anywhere. The softly spoken endearment made her bones quiver. The ground tilted beneath her feet.

Rosie had to force herself to turn and face him. She knew what damage it could do to the semblance of equilibrium she'd been nurturing all day.

She'd been so right to be afraid, she acknowledged on an inner sob of despair. He was so beautiful. Moonlight threw the planes of his face into harsh relief, tumbled in his endearingly rumpled hair, darkened the tanned skin which was already emphasised by the white shirt that clung to his wide shoulders. She would love this man to the end of time, forgive him anything; there lay the danger.

Knowing she had to fight it, remind herself that all she'd ever been to him was a willing partner in a furtive sexual fling, she gathered her defences and stated calmly, 'You startled me. I thought you weren't expected back until tomorrow.'

'I was impatient to return.'

He was close enough for her to feel his body heat, to inhale the heady male scent of him. His lean, fantastically sexy body was tautly held, and she wished he wasn't so impossibly gorgeous, so utterly tempting…

'Do you want to know the reason for my impatience?' His eyes glittered beneath the dark, heavy fringe of lashes. 'Shall I tell you?'

Tension spiralled inside her. When he looked at her like that, one dark brow indolently raised, a smile playing at the corners of his sensual mouth, and spoke in that low, sexy undertone, she just flipped. Already she could feel hot colour flooding over her face.

Self-defensively, she turned away. 'I can guess.' Was that shaky squawk her voice? Dabbling her fingers in the cool water that trickled from the fountain into a wide, heavily carved bowl, she pulled in a breath and managed calmly, 'You can relax. I'm not pregnant. And I'm as pleased about it as you must be,' she tacked on hurriedly, just in case he thought she found the news unwelcome because she'd wanted to have some hold over him, trap him maybe.

She couldn't see his face, of course, but he was probably grinning from ear to ear with relief. But when he eventually spoke after moments of silence that made her spine prickle, he sounded sort of heavy.

'If that's what you really feel, then we must take more care in future.'

Future? What future?

An on/off furtive affair? Someone he could count on for no-strings sexual release whenever he happened to visit the UK? She might, for her sins, love the brute, but she would not be seduced into being his bit on the side! Or was he really going to ask her to marry him, as he'd told Terrina he would?

'Forget it!' She whirled round on her heels, glaring up into his hard, implacable features. 'I don't intend to jump into bed with you whenever you're around and happen to feel the urge! But at least your offer—if that was what it was—means you've stopped being so darn ratty!' she finished on a humiliating wobble. Dammit all, she was crying again! When would she learn to grow up and be adult enough to hide her emotions?

'Stop it, Rosie!' Sebastian commanded rawly, his hands curving heavily around her shoulders. 'Don't cry. *Idiota!* I was never angry with you—or only for a few shocked moments when I stupidly thought you were spinning a line when you claimed to be Marcus's daughter. And I did apologise for that, remember? Remember?' he reiterated firmly, giving her a gentle shake when she refused to answer.

'You shouldn't have believed that, not even for a moment!' she objected thickly. 'You really hurt me, you know that?'

They had spent such a perfect evening and night together and she'd really dared to believe that he was beginning to feel something more than just lust for her. Then he'd made her whole world fall apart by accusing her of being out for what she hoped she could get.

'I'm sorry, *cara mia*, I hope you will some day forgive me for a momentary lack of trust.' He looped an arm around her shoulders and led her to a seat in a corner of the courtyard, beneath an arbour covered with wisteria, designed to give shade in the heat of the day. 'Sit and listen to my confession.'

He settled beside her and took her hands in his. Rosie smartly released them, sensing real danger. He only had to touch her to have every sensible thought flying out of her head. She fished in the pocket of her stylish jacket for a tissue and blew her nose.

Loudly.

Hopefully, her elephantine trumpeting would put him off his stride, stop him from seducing her disastrously weak self into agreeing to his dubious and disgracefully demeaning plans for her future.

It didn't have the desired effect. Even here, in the shadows where the moonlight didn't reach, she could see him smile. And his hand as he brushed her hair away from her overheated forehead was bone-shakingly tender.

'I was nineteen when I fell in love for the first time,' he told her quietly. 'Looking back, I know it was just a sudden rush of the rioting hormones that young men are prone to. I met Magdalena in a night-club. She was absolutely stunning. And when she made a direct play for me I was so flattered, so puffed up with pride, I could barely stand upright! I was so besotted I did everything she asked of me—bought her anything that took her fancy, squired her to the best restaurants, brought her home to meet my parents. You name it, Magdalena got it.

'That weekend we spent here she got careless. She wrote a postcard to her sister in Madrid and asked Tomas to post it. She hadn't bargained on the average human being's curiosity. Tomas read it and brought it to me. In essence, it was boasting about her divine luck. She'd landed a rich idiot. Five years her junior and still wet enough behind the ears to be as malleable as putty. That weekend, at his fancy home, she was going to get an engagement ring out of him and then she'd be home and dry and looking forward to a life of luxury.

'After that, I have to admit, I got cynical,' he continued with a self-deprecating shrug of his wide shoulders. 'Especially when I met more of her kind over the ensuing years. Glossily packaged women trading on their looks, with their eyes on the main chance. And that, *cara*, will explain—not excuse—why my hard-nosed cynicism made me overreact when you told me who you were.' He took her hands in his again and this time she made no attempt to remove them, mesmerised by what he had told her, even pitying him and the circumstances of great wealth, not to mention fabulous good looks, that had made him so wary of women and their motives. It had turned him into a cynic, too, she thought sadly. His only interest the acquisition of more and more wealth.

'And as for being ratty, as you put it, my anger wasn't directed towards you, *mia cara*, but against Marcus for what I perceived as a double betrayal—against Tia Lucia and your abandoned mother. For the life of hardship you and she had to bear. When I actually listened to what he had to say I understood and could finally sympathise.'

'You only thought about what you call the "double betrayal" when you began to believe that I might really have proof of my identity. To begin with, your immediate thought was of my father's money,' she accused miserably, hating to have to think so badly of him.

'For that I am sorry. I have told you. Explained why I became so mistrustful. Please forgive me.'

Rosie mentally stiffened her spine. If she allowed herself to weaken she could easily agree to become his occasional mistress, if only to prove to him that this woman could love him for what he was, not for the depth of his pocket.

Yet something was niggling at the back of her mind and, try as she might, flustered as her emotions were, she couldn't access it.

Until the pressure of his lean fingers on hers increased and he said in a driven undertone, 'Marry me, Rosie. I want you for my wife.'

She felt as if she'd been hit by a ton of bricks. She'd been dreading this, really hoping that he wasn't so self-seeking as to go this far. Terrina's words punched fiery holes in her brain and pushed daggers through her heart: 'You'd better get your skates on and slap a wedding ring on his new-found daughter's finger, hadn't you? It's the only way to make sure of your future inheritance.'

The smooth-tongued, manipulative louse hadn't wasted any time, had he? How could he do this to her? He was no better than that—whatever her name was—who had tried to trap him into marriage for mercenary reasons all those years ago!

With a monumental effort, considering how closely her legs resembled a half-set jelly, she made it to her feet. And her voice was all raggedy as she got out, 'Get lost, Sebastian! And if you value your eyesight you'll never come near me again!'

And stumbled back into the house. And got lost all over again. When, half blinded by the ridiculous tears she had no sensible reason for shedding, she located her room, she only had time to lock the door behind her and crumple into a heap of misery on the floor before his imperious knock came. His tense request that she open it. Right now.

She ignored it. The carved door was stout. He'd need an axe to gain entry.

She would ignore him and whatever he said or did for the rest of her life!

Strange how that resolution brought her no comfort at all.

CHAPTER TWELVE

GOING through the motions, Rosie showered, dressed in a sleek cream linen skirt and topped it with a light silk-knit overblouse, did her make-up and forced herself out into the small courtyard where breakfast, so she'd been told, was taken in fine weather.

Marcus and Elvira were already seated at the white cloth-covered table in the shade of a gnarled fig tree, and as her father rose to his feet, his face a bright welcome, Rosie determinedly returned his smile.

Today was a new beginning. In turning down Sebastian's cynical proposal in no uncertain manner, listening to his impatient footsteps retreating down the corridor last night, she'd become stronger, in charge of her own destiny, far less likely to jump when he decided to tweak her strings.

'Good morning, my dear—we have another beautiful day.' Elvira's greeting was just as welcoming. Rosie agreed that, yes, it was, and took a vacant seat, a warm glow melting the block of ice that had been her heart. It was wonderful to feel she was accepted. It went some way towards cancelling out Sebastian's coldly calculating manipulations.

The table was set with jugs of iced juice, pots of coffee, hot rolls wrapped in linen napkins, pots of conserve and a dish of sliced tomatoes sprinkled with fresh herbs. Rosie's stomach closed up as she helped herself to coffee, willing the hand that held the pot not to shake.

Elvira laid down her napkin and got to her feet, very smart this morning in a light grey tailored suit, her dark hair coiled in a glossy knot at her nape. 'I'm afraid you'll have to excuse me, but duty calls. I have a committee meeting in Jerez—a worthwhile charity. Have either of you seen my son this morning?'

Was her gaze, her query, directed mainly at her? Had Elvira guessed that there was more to her relationship with Sebastian than his self-appointed mission to deliver her to her father?

Willing herself not to blush, Rosie shook her head, and at her father's negative reply she wondered if, after last night's put-down, he'd taken himself off to sulk and grumble at himself for the lost opportunity to secure his future inheritance.

She sincerely hoped so, even if a wayward and regrettably treacherous part of her missed him. It would be easier on her if she never had to set eyes on him again.

'What would you like to do today?' Relaxed, his smile indulgent, Marcus leant back in his chair. 'Anything you like, sweetheart. Drive to the coast? Explore Jerez, Cadiz? Or we could try to get a flight back to England—I can't wait to get you back home. Think about it. We can revisit Spain at our leisure whenever you like.'

Which would be never!

'Going home sounds great.' Rosie was sure she meant it, any doubts swept away by the beam of satisfaction on her father's face. Besides, looked at sensibly, putting a great deal of distance between herself and Sebastian was the best way of dealing with this situation.

'You finish your breakfast, sweetheart, while I make a phone call. We may have to wait a day or two, but I'll book us on the first available flight.'

Marcus was already on his feet when Sebastian strode purposefully towards them. Dressed in a crisp white shirt tucked into narrow dark trousers, he looked so handsome it was terrifying.

Rosie's heartbeat accelerated and her stomach convulsed as she watched like a mesmerised rabbit while he addressed Marcus, his proud head high, his features expressionless, as he stated, 'Marcus, sir, I would like your permission to ask for your daughter's hand in marriage.'

In the shocking silence that followed that outlandish request Rosie could cheerfully have throttled him. Then she just wanted to curl up and die! This was so humiliating!

'I see.' Marcus dragged his pop-eyed stare from Sebastian's steely silver eyes and grinned down at Rosie. 'So that's the way the wind blows—I had wondered!' He harummphed gruffly. 'Go to it, my boy! I'll make myself scarce. I'll be with the morning papers, should you need me.'

'How could you?' Rosie was on her feet, quivering with outrage as soon as her father was safely out of earshot. 'You've just made huge fools out of us both. Nobody does that ridiculous formal stuff!'

Straddle-legged, he thrust his hands into his trouser pockets, his left eyebrow arching upwards, his slight smile as sultry as his voice. 'I got him on my side, didn't I?'

'So? What good will that do you? I've already turned you down.'

'Why?' He advanced a pace. Rosie retreated. The palms of her hands itched to slap him.

'Marry me, Rosie. You know you want to.' A long stride forward. He was really close now. She could touch him if she wanted to. She didn't. Or only with a heavy brick!

Frozen to the spot by his sheer audacity, she could only fling her head back on her slender neck and treat him to her fiercest glare, impressing, finally, she hoped, her, 'No!'

'Why?'

Persistent devil! Those lancet-silver eyes were boring holes right through her. Outrage flowed away as suddenly as it had arisen, leaving her feeling horribly empty. She knew, to her abiding shame, that if he took her in his arms, held her, he would have won. She would take him on any terms at all because life without him would be unbearable.

But she was made of sterner stuff, wasn't she? Besides, he made no move to touch her, which the weaker part of her regretted very much indeed. But at least it meant she could still fight her corner, give him the answer he was seeking, the reason why any woman on the planet would turn down the catch of the decade!

'You proposed marriage only because Terrina told you you should. I might fancy you rotten—well, you know that, or should do,' she mumbled, lowering her head because she was suddenly overcome with shame over how sordid it all seemed. 'But I won't marry you just because you think my father will disinherit you and leave everything to me.'

She risked a quick upward glance. His dark brows were knotted irately. Because his true motivations had been pushed under his nose?

Her battered heart twisted violently inside her with pity. How dreadful to be so hooked on money you had to scheme and play dirty to get even more of the stuff. 'I wouldn't worry about it too much,' she offered in wobbly-voiced consolation. 'Marcus has known and loved you all of your life. He's only known of my existence for a day and a bit. Besides,' she added earnestly, because that frown showed no sign of lightening, 'I've already told him I want nothing from him except the right to call him my father.'

'Rosie—' A muscle jerked at the side of his tough jawline. His hands shot out to pinion her narrow shoulders. 'You've been talking to Terrina.'

'A bit,' she admitted sadly. How strange; she didn't hate him, after all. She felt so sorry for him she could feel the tears of sympathy well up behind her eyes. Being found out must be hard for a proud man to swallow. 'She did ask me to get you away from here because she was afraid you were trying to split her and Marcus up. If they married, she said, her husband's property would go to her and not to you. Though, personally, I think it's pretty sordid to think of things like that when you're in love with someone and planning a wedding.'

Groaning something in his own language, Sebastian gave her a melting smile. '*Querida*, you are something else! Not a mean or sneaky bone in that beautiful body or a nasty thought in that lovely head. That was what made me fall in love with you.'

Rosie's eyes glazed over and her heart bumped around inside her chest. She said sorrowfully, 'You don't have to use the "love" word.' She would have given anything to believe that he meant it, but she couldn't fool herself. She didn't want to hurt his pride any more than it already was, but it had to be said. 'There's more. I overheard your conversation the night before she left. You told her she had to go. I think you were giving her money. It sounded as if you were blackmailing her. And I heard her telling you to put a ring on my finger to make sure you didn't lose out on your inheritance. And then you said that was what you intended to do. And I think that's just horrible!'

'Ah.' A speaking silence and then a whirl of activity as he swung a chair round from the table, sat down, and pulled her on to his knee. 'I had to get rid of her. Not on my account. Marcus is a wealthy man, but my family could buy him out many times over. Besides, I'd far rather have him around than receive anything he might or might not leave in his will! But the Terrinas of this world don't think like that. She obviously translated her own greedy motives on to me. As far as I was concerned, she could have had everything if she could have made him happy.'

Staunchly fighting the impulse to cuddle closer, lie against him in the haven of the strong arms that were just lightly enclosing her, Rosie demanded, 'How do you know she wouldn't have made him happy?'

A long finger traced the quivering outline of her mouth. Rosie's insides quivered in sympathy as she quelled the desire to take that same ravaging finger between her lips.

'Because she lied to him,' Sebastian spelt out heavily. 'She wheedled her way into his affections—I had to watch it happen. Telling lies about her desire to have a family when I know for a gold-plated fact that she can never have children.' His voice roughened in disgust. 'It's a small world, Rosie, uncomfortably small sometimes. Terrina was trawling the circuit—doing the rounds of all the ''in'' places,' he added by way of explanation, 'long before she met Marcus on the golf course. A few years ago, a friend of mine had the misfortune to get tangled up with her. He wasn't husband material—not nearly rich or important enough—but he was useful to take her to places where she could hopefully cast her net to catch bigger fish. She got pregnant. Much to my friend's distress she went for an abortion. As I've said, if he'd been loaded she'd have had the baby, used it as a bargaining chip. But he wasn't, so the baby had to go. Something went wrong. It left her unable to have children.'

He closed his eyes, and the look that crossed his face wasn't what Rosie would call comfortable. She touched his face with the cool length of her fingers, her darkened eyes understanding as he turned his head and put a kiss in her palm. 'I'm not proud of what I had to do. Pay her off. Unfortunately for her, I was one of the few people who knew the truth. I couldn't stand by and let Marcus be led by the nose. She'd got him believing that she was dying to present him with a nursery full of babies. He might not have loved her, but he did become fond of her because she flattered him and gave him the belief that he had a second chance to have a family of his own.'

'You did the right thing!' Rosie was horrified to think how badly that dreadful woman could have hurt and disappointed her father. 'But,' she added thoughtfully, 'she must be a very unhappy woman, so we mustn't blame her too much.' She framed his face with loving hands, consoling him. 'Your mother said Marcus wasn't upset. He was more relieved than anything when Terrina left him. So you mustn't worry about having to blackmail her. And maybe she'll have learned her lesson and one day she'll meet someone she can love for himself. And if they want children, they could adopt, couldn't they?' she queried brightly, already dreaming up a happier future for the woman who could have hurt her father so badly.

Silver eyes narrowed. 'I can understand you being sorry for Terrina—you're that sort of woman. But you're sorry for me, too!' He sounded as if that happening was utterly outrageous.

'Yes, of course I am.' Rosie tilted her blonde head on one side and gave him a small, sorrowful smile. 'You might be wildly handsome, and huge in the wealth department, but you are only human. And human beings have consciences, and yours is probably uncomfortable right now, so—'

Silencing whatever she might be coming out with next with a blistering string of Spanish oaths, Sebastian shot to his feet, planting her firmly down in front of him. Then, after a withering silence, he gave her an unreadable look.

He released his breath slowly. 'Do you pity me

enough to marry me and put me out of my misery? Would the kindness of your heart extend that far?'

There was a tight line around his sensual mouth that suggested all kinds of devastating reactions if she gave the wrong answer. Her soft mouth prim, she regarded him levelly. She now knew that the role of blackmailer didn't fit him easily, that he'd gritted his teeth and got on with it for the sake of his godfather. And as for wanting to marry her for whatever she might inherit in the future, well, that didn't seem likely, either. As he'd explained, that was the way Terrina's mind worked, not his.

'No,' she answered, figuring honesty was the best policy. 'No, I wouldn't. I would only marry you if I knew you really loved me.' She gulped round the lump in her throat.

Her heart trembled, then picked up speed as he reached for her hands and pressed ardent kisses in both small palms. 'Love you? I adore you!'

'Really?'

Ecstatic happiness stirred inside her and exploded into a starburst of joy as he crushed her in his arms, murmuring against her hair, 'I swear on my life I will love you for ever. I wanted you from the minute I saw you. *Querida*, I was slow on the uptake. I didn't recognise love until I worked out my reasons for needing to keep you with me. We could have done that simple pregnancy test—I'd already decided I'd take my responsibilities seriously and marry you if you were carrying my child—there was no real reason for keeping you under my eye until nature took its course. The real reason, of course, was that I couldn't bear to let you out of my sight, out of my life.'

That made the most glorious sense, she recognised. They'd both been fighting what they felt for each other for far too long. 'I love you so much!' She angled her head so that she could look up into his precious face and saw sudden radiance flare in his beautiful eyes.

'And you will marry me.'

More a statement than a question, but she answered anyway. 'Yes.'

The kiss that sealed their commitment left them both breathless. Sebastian slid his fingers through her hair, positioning his mouth above hers again, and stressed, 'To clear up any lingering doubts, *cara mia*, when you dropped that bombshell about who you were, it pushed us in another direction. I'd been on the point of asking you to be my wife. Not as a future heiress, but as the cleaning lady with scarcely a rag to her back and barely a bean in her purse! I love you for what you are—utterly adorable, loving, open-hearted, sexy, the most radiantly beautiful—'

Rosie kissed him to stem the flow of compliments because they were making her ears burn. They couldn't possibly be true, or only to him, and surely that was all that mattered. And just as surely she was going to make certain he thought that way for the rest of his life.

Two months later, on a balmy day in May, they were married from Troone Manor. As Rosie swept down the aisle on her proud father's arm, wearing a dream of a dress in pale cream-coloured wild silk, she knew she was about to burst with happiness. The immaculately suited groom turned to watch her, and there was so much love in his silver eyes she just melted and had to hang on to her father's arm for dear life to stop herself from swooning clean away.

This morning's test had proved positive! She would give Sebastian the good tidings while they drove back to the Manor for the lavish reception.

After she'd agreed to marry him there had been so many toings and froings her head had been permanently spinning. Back here to England, then back to Cadiz to Sebastian's home—a beautiful place to have conceived his child—then back to Troone to plan the wedding, culminating in this special occasion, the joining of two loving souls.

Their eyes meshed as she took her place beside him. The glow of love in his made her heart swell in delight. She sought his hand, their fingers entwining. 'I will never stop loving you,' Sebastian whispered, and knew he'd never said a truer word.

Become a Panel Member

If YOU are a regular United Kingdom buyer of Mills & Boon® Modern Romance™ or Tender Romance™ you might like to tell us your opinion of the books we publish to help us in publishing the books *you* like. Mills & Boon have a Reader Panel of Modern and Tender Romance readers. Each person on the panel receives a short questionnaire (taking about five minutes to complete) every third month asking for opinions of the past month's Modern and Tender Romances. All people who send in their replies have a chance of winning a FREE year's supply of Modern or Tender Romances.
If YOU would like to be considered for inclusion on the panel please fill in and return the following survey. We can't guarantee that everyone will be on the panel but first come will be first considered.

Where did you buy this novel?

- ❑ WH Smith
- ❑ Tesco
- ❑ Borders
- ❑ Sainsbury's
- ❑ Direct by mail
- ❑ Other (please state) ________________________

What themes do you enjoy most in the Mills & Boon® novels that you read? (Choose all that apply.)

- ❑ Amnesia
- ❑ Family drama (including babies/young children)
- ❑ Hidden/Mistaken identity
- ❑ Historical setting
- ❑ Marriage of convenience
- ❑ Modern or Tender drama
- ❑ Mediterranean men
- ❑ Millionaire heroes
- ❑ Mock engagement or marriage
- ❑ Outback setting
- ❑ Revenge
- ❑ Sheikh heroes

- ❑ Secret baby
- ❑ Shared pasts
- ❑ Western
- ❑ Forced proximity
- ❑ Mistress heroines

On average, how many Mills & Boon® novels do you read every month?____________________

Please provide us with your name and address:

Name: ____
Address: ______________________________________

What is your occupation?
(OPTIONAL)

In which of the following age groups do you belong?
(OPTIONAL)

- ❑ 18 to 24
- ❑ 25 to 34
- ❑ 35 to 49
- ❑ 50 to 64
- ❑ 65 or older

Thank you for your help!
Your feedback is important in helping us offer quality products you value.

The Reader Service
Reader Panel Questionnaire
FREEPOST CN81
Croydon CR9 3WZ

MODRD502

MODERN SURVEY B